FATAL WIN

FATAL WIN

SAMANTHA SHAW

iUniverse, Inc.
Bloomington

FATAL WIN

iUniverse books may be ordered through booksellers or by contacting:

iUniverse
1663 Liberty Drive
Bloomington, IN 47403
www.iuniverse.com
1-800-Authors (1-800-288-4677)

ISBN: 978-1-4697-9494-5 (sc)
ISBN: 978-1-4697-9495-2 (ebk)

Printed in the United States of America

iUniverse rev. date: 03/08/2012

CHAPTER ONE

The ocean was unusually calm as he walked in. Cold too. Lawrence Taylor took a moment then dove headfirst into the icy, tranquil water. He began to swim and noticed he was the only one around. Perfect. The sun was just beginning to set and he felt privileged to be the only one to witness it, to be part of it. He floated on his back and closed his eyes, drifting far, far away from shore. When he finally opened them, he could barely make out the shoreline in the distance. Panicked, he began to quickly swim towards it. Suddenly, out of nowhere, he felt something bite down hard on his leg and attempt to pull him under. The water turned a bright, crimson red. Shark! Larry began to scream, hoping somehow someone would hear him and come to his rescue. The cold, salty water surged over his head as he was slowly pulled under.

Then he heard it. A whistle! He struggled with all his remaining strength and his head managed to break through the water. Through bleary eyes he saw what looked like a lifeguard running towards the shore. The man was blowing his whistle while motioning help was on its way. The very last thing Larry remembered was hearing the whistle blowing as the shark pulled him down towards the ocean bottom. Lower and lower and lower . . .

Startled, Larry woke up. His heart was racing but it was only a dream. He was safely in his bed and the telephone on the nightstand beside him was ringing.

"Yeah," Larry barked into it. But whoever it was had hung up. Actually, Larry knew who it was. Who else would be calling him after midnight? It was Bob no doubt, his so-called best friend and party animal, probably calling him to come join yet another all night party. Well forget it. Larry had enough of wild parties to last him a lifetime. He was forty and all partied out. Besides, he had other things on his mind.

Completely naked, he crawled out of bed and decided to go into the kitchen. On his way he couldn't resist turning on the lights and confronting himself in the full-length mirror. Did he really look forty? He didn't think so. He had a great body and a full head of wavy, jet-black hair, though a few grays had found their way into it recently. That's what they had hair color for, wasn't it? All in all, he was rather handsome. Too bad his mind was failing.

He was a mental mess. Stressed out to the max. And it wasn't coming from his sales position at the Boston office of Ideal Advertising.

Actually, he taught he could handle his growing anxiety if it weren't for all the dreams regarding death. His death. They were slowly killing him. Last night he had dreamed he was set upon by a pack of wild animals that were mutilating him, tearing apart his flesh with their razor sharp teeth. The night before he had a nightmare of a teenage gangs terrorizing him, drenching his body with gasoline and setting him on fire.

Every night a new scenario from hell tormented him. It was becoming so he was afraid to go to sleep. Because of this he spent most the day in a trance-like state, walking around like some drugged out zombie.

Even Peter Jenkins, that nosy bartender at The Post bar had noticed how frazzled Larry had become. The jerk even had the nerve to suggest Larry see a psychiatrist.

Imagine that. Fat chance of that ever happening. It would be a cold day in hell before he'd ever consult a shrink. Why should he? It wasn't like he was schizo or anything.

More importantly, what good would it do? Last time Larry checked, there was no cure for this thing called life.

In a daze, he stumbled into the kitchen and grabbed a six-pack out of the refrigerator. He popped open a can and sat down at the table, drinking the cold beer and welcoming the relief the alcohol would provide. Damn it! He could still feel the shark biting into his leg and dragging him beneath the water to his death. Thank God it was only a dream. He popped open a second can of beer and guzzled it down too. If he drank enough maybe he could still catch a few hours of sleep. The last thing he wanted was for his supervisor, Mr. Josh Hillman, to notice how stressed out he'd become.

The ringing of the telephone pierced the silence. "Hello," Larry slurred into it.

"Hey, buddy. What are you doing? I tried calling earlier but there was no answer."

Sure enough, it was Bob, his best friend. "I was trying to sleep."

"Sleep? That's a dirty word where I come from. Besides, you can sleep anytime. There's a crowd of us at The Post and we're having a great time drinking it up. Come join us."

"Not tonight," Larry yawned.

"Party pooper. What's the matter with you lately? You seem, well, preoccupied, not your old partying self."

"I'm O.K."

"Sure. And the sky is pink. You gonna join us or not?"

"Not tonight. Another time, maybe."

"Whatever you say. I gotta go. I'll call you next time around. You're missing a great time, you know. You could really score tonight."

"Whatever. I just can't make it tonight."

"Your loss," Bob hung up the phone.

"Perhaps," Larry said as he hung up the phone. Life was one big party to Bob. It was only recently it stopped being so for Larry. Was that a sure sign of getting old or what?

Sleep. That's what he really needed before he passed out somewhere. It took the entire six-pack to mellow him out sufficiently to return back to bed. He lay there tensely, daring himself to close his eyes. He could sense another nightmare within him just seeking release.

With great apprehension, Lawrence Taylor finally drifted off into a troubled sleep.

Victoria Moore let out a long, exhaustive sigh. It had been a difficult morning. Not only had she lost her wallet with all her credit cards in it, but also her right heel had twisted off as she ran to catch the downtown Boston trolley, forcing her to limp aboard the crowded vehicle. But what really got her going was the idiot who began rubbing up against her once she was standing inside. As a newly practicing psychiatrist she had been trained to handle and confront all sorts of difficult situations, but now she was not sure what to do. She attempted to move into the car, but there was very little room in which to maneuver. Once again she felt the rubber brush up against her, his hot, stale breath burning the back of her neck. She bit her tongue. With one more stop remaining to her destination of Park Street, she convinced herself she could hang in there without confronting the guy and possibly making her late for her ten o'clock appointment. Suddenly she heard the guy making whimpering noises behind her. A wave of nausea and anger swept over her small frame. My God, he's having and orgasm! she realized.

"Park Street—Last stop," the conductor called as a sea of humanity rushed towards the now open doors. With great effort, Vicki spun around to confront the rubber. Surprisingly he was quite young with an angelic face, but Vicki was clearly able to see the wet spot on the front of his jeans before he quickly moved his backpack over it.

She began to tremble. Before she could stop herself, she felt her left leg, the one still with a heel, rise and with all the strength she could muster come down hard on his right sneaker. He yelped and the backpack fell from his hand, exposing the wet spot for all to see.

With a smile of satisfaction, Vicki exited the trolley. Once inside the station, she pounded her left shoe against an empty bench until the heel came off. Now both shoes were heel-less, but at least she could walk somewhat normally. Looking around the station, the young man who had so invaded her privacy was nowhere in sight. Just as well, Vicki figured, as she probably would have told him off after all. She quickly ran her hands over her slacks to make sure none of the wetness had gotten on them and then joined the crowd making a rush towards the nearest escalator.

Only once outside did Vicki let herself relax. She hated riding the subway on a good day, and this was definitely not a good day.

She wobbled across the street to where her office was at 128 Tremont. It was an old building, practically falling apart. Because of its age and history, the city of Boston had decided it couldn't be sold or torn down, but had no money to fix it either. But Vicki loved it anyway. Just as the elevator door opened on the fifth floor was her office. It was a modest office with a small waiting area. Inside the office, comfortable leather chairs surrounded a small coffee table. In the corner was a large bookcase holding psychiatry texts. But by far the best part of the office was the huge bay window overlooking Boston Common. It had a fantastic view of the State House. Vicki loved the view, but her patients seemed mesmerized by it, often spending most of a session staring out at the Common and the people below. Vicki realized coming for treatment was difficult and made most people very nervous. She felt the view offered her patients the opportunity to somewhat escape mentally, which was fine with her. The more comfortable people felt, the more they'd open up, which was one reason she kept a coffee machine and small refrigerator filled with cold drinks in the corner. She wanted her clients to feel they could make a cup of coffee or grab a juice at any time during the session.

The answering machine on a stand near the coffee machine was blinking and she went to it to see who had called. One message was from Mark Potter, who was calling to cancel his ten o'clock session.

Vicki sighed. The next message was from Peter Jenkins, a bartender at The Post bar in town she was treating for manic depression. He had called to tell her that he recommended Lawrence Taylor, who was a regular customer at The Post, call her for an appointment.

Realizing that was her last message, Vicki reset the machine. She had an hour to kill and decided to go downtown and buy a new pair of shoes. She spent most of it at Baker's Shoe Store trying on various styles but ultimately decided on a pair of brown leather sandals. She'd have to hurry if she wanted to be on time for her next appointment.

Quickly she paid for them with some money she had stashed in her handbag. Not looking where she was going, she rushed out of the store.

WHAM! She collided right into a man drinking a can of diet Pepsi. The can went flying out of his hand, completely drenching him in the process.

"I'm so sorry," Vicki apologized for her clumsiness. The morning had just progressed from bad to worse. "I think I have some tissues in my bag," she muttered as she opened her small handbag and fumbled through it.

"It's okay. Really," the stranger insisted, shaking off whatever Pepsi he could from his clothes.

"Here they are!" Vicki announced triumphantly, handing him several crumpled tissues. For the first time since the encounter their eyes met and Vicki realized how handsome this stranger was. He had wavy black hair, high cheekbones and a really nice smile.

"At least let me pay for your dry cleaning bill," Vicki insisted.

"Don't worry about it," the man told her. "It's no big deal. I have another shirt I can change into at work. No harm done. Thanks for the tissues," he added as he walked away.

Vicki watched as he disappeared into the crowd at Downtown Crossing. He was the most handsome man she had seen in a long time and she had to admit she was more than a little attracted to him. A part of her wished to shout after him, ask him for a date or a phone number or something, but that was not her style.

Knowing she'd never see him again and she was dating Dave Weyes, a fellow psychiatrist, she headed back to her office where one of her most difficult patients would be waiting. Carrie Graden was a young woman whom Vicki had diagnosed suffering from borderline personality disorder.

Though only twenty-three, Carrie had tried to kill herself and was only recently released from MMI—the Massachusetts Mental Institute. It was Vicki's fear that one day Carrie would succeed in killing herself.

Carrie was in the waiting room when Vicki opened her office and escorted her in.

"How are you feeling today?" Vicki asked.

"Good."

"You don't look like you're doing too good."

"I'm doing just great. Leave me alone."

"Attempting suicide is a serious matter. Why don't we talk about some of the things that led up to you feeling so desperate."

"I don't want to. Fuck off."

"It's important we identify what led up to your suicide attempt so we can learn to prevent you feeling so desperate in the future," Vicki tried to explain. It was necessary to find out what had prompted Carrie to swallow approximately sixty Seconals along with a pint of Vodka. She was lucky to be alive.

"Why do we have to bother to identify anything? Why isn't it enough that I just don't want to live? Life sucks. This whole world sucks. The whole fucking universe sucks. End of story."

"What sucks about the universe?"

"Absolutely everything."

"Like what, Carrie."

"Fuck you. I don't want to talk with you."

It went like that for the entire hour: Vicki attempting to elicit a straight answer and Carrie refusing to give one. With the session ending without any results, Vicki scheduled Carrie to come in twice a week. Maybe with them meeting more often, Carrie would open up. The suicide attempt served as an indication to Vicki just how seriously ill Carrie was. All she could do was hope that a part of Carrie still remained motivated to get well. That was the part Vicki was trying to reach.

Vicki was feeling tired by the time she locked her office door for the night and headed home. She had seen six more patients after Carrie and was frustrated at the lack of progress each was making. A part of her wanted to sit and chat with them, to be their friend, yet she knew she must remain cool, aloof and impersonal. She could never show just how much she cared beyond her cold, professional exterior. Trouble was, she did care. Very much.

She had always been the caring, sensitive one. Born to a family of seven in England, she earned that title at a young age when her parents noticed she was somehow different than the others. Vicki would hate it when her mother would introduce her and then say 'she's the sensitive one.' But slowly she began to see it as an asset; a badge of honor. It meant that she was alive, that she felt things and cared deeply. While attending medical school at Harvard, they had assured her these were good qualities to have in her chosen career. Yet whenever a patient stumbled, she felt herself personally feeling hurt and frustrated, like today.

In time I'll learn to handle these feelings better, Vicki told herself as she climbed down the stairs to Park Street Station below. A trolley pulled up and opened its doors and Vicki joined the other people jostling and pushing to get on board. Because it was after rush hour, Vicki even found a seat.

She must have dozed off for twenty minutes for when she opened her eyes the trolley was traveling outside and no longer in the tunnel. Since the next stop was where she wanted to get off, Vicki stood up and slowly edged her way towards the doors. With a loud, screeching noise the trolley came to a stop and Vicki alighted, crossing the street to her apartment building. College-town. That's what they called this section of Brighton because of all the college students living there. Even though she was no longer a student, Vicki gave but scant attention to moving. She loved it in Brighton. There was always something going on.

Vicki climbed the stairs leading to her second story apartment as she fumbled for the key. Finally she found it buried in the corner of her handbag underneath some old candy wrappers and tampons. I really should clean this bag, she considered as she inserted the key and opened the door.

It felt good to be home after a long day and Vicki quickly changed into something more comfortable. Then she raided the refrigerator for an apple and went over to play the messages people had left on her home phone answering machine. There was only one message and it was from Dave. "Vicki, please give me a call when you get in. Ciao."

Vicki sighed. She had met Dave at a professional function a year ago. He was a staff psychiatrist at the New England People's Hospital and make it clear he thought very highly of this position. They had been dating off and on, but Vicki's heart wasn't into the relationship. There was something about Dave's personality she just didn't like. But Dave was persistent, calling her with more and more frequency and turning up the pressure to further their relationship. He desired to date her exclusively, but she kept putting up obstacles to avoid making that commitment.

As far as she was concerned, she was just unlucky when it came to men. It was that simple. It wasn't because she was unattractive. In fact, most men loved her long blonde hair and green eyes. She looked years younger than her age of thirty-eight and often had to show some identification before buying wine or alcoholic beverages. In college and throughout her internship she had dated many men, not even coming close to finding one she remotely liked. Unfortunately, Dave was turning out no different. Once Vicki had even sat down with paper and pen forcing herself to write down all of Dave's good qualities. She couldn't think of any.

This is ridiculous, she finally decided. The problem was with her. It was that she was too much of a perfectionist. There was absolutely nothing wrong with Dave. She picked up the phone and called him back.

"Hello," his voice sounded out of breath.

"Hi," Vicki said, trying to keep her voice upbeat.

"Vicki! You just caught me coming out of the shower. Hold on."

She played with the phone cord trying to convince herself she actually liked Dave.

"Sorry to keep you waiting. How about I pick up a bottle of wine and come right over?"

"Naw. Tonight's no good. I have to work tomorrow."

"So don't I and you don't hear me complaining. C'mon. I need to unwind a bit. I'll be over in an hour."

Vicki started to say something only to realize Dave had already hung up. So much for a quiet evening home alone. Her stomach growled and she realized other that the apple she hadn't eaten since the sandwich she had at noon. If Dave hadn't hung up so quickly she would have told him to pick up some Chinese food or a pizza or something.

An hour later Dave pounded on the door. "Did you miss me," he grinned at Vicki the second she opened it.

"Yeah," Vicki said with hardly any enthusiasm. "Why'd you hang up on me like that for? I'm starving. I was going to tell you to bring over some take-out food. Besides some apples, all I have in the house is a box of macaroni and cheese."

"Yuck," Dave made a face. He hated macaroni and cheese. "Sorry for hanging up on you, but I wanted to get here as soon as possible. I even forgot to pick up some wine. Let me make it up to you by taking you to dinner."

"Sounds great," Vicki said, considering it a good idea. If he had brought over wine and food, he'd probably be clamoring for sex afterward. "Let's go. I'm ready," Vicki grabbed a sweater in case the evening was a cool one.

"Not so fast," Dave smiled seductively. "I just remembered something. I haven't given you a kiss yet."

That's okay, Vicki thought mentally.

He pulled her close to him, holding her head as his lips sought out hers. It was a wet kiss, hot and electrifying. Vicki felt his hard bulge press against her stomach.

"You feel so good," he whimpered into her ear, gyrating his hardness against her just as the young man on the trolley had earlier. If Vicki didn't act quickly, they were going to wind up having sex after all.

"What's the matter?" Dave felt her pull back.

"Nothing. I'm just real hungry." She was in no mood to sleep with Dave.

"Too hungry to even make love?" Dave took her by the hand and led her into the bedroom.

They wound up making love after all, despite the fact she didn't want to. It usually went this way. Soon, Vicki swore, she'd find a way to break off with Dave like she had with all her other boyfriends. It was just hard for her to initiate the conversation leading to the break-up. She eventually found the words, but it was never easy for her to reject anyone. It wasn't in her nature.

"So where would you like to go eat?" Dave asked her, finally satisfied. He got out of bed and began to put his clothes on.

"Let's try that new restaurant at Copley Place called The Emperor. One of my patients had eaten there and said it was good."

"The Emperor it is," Dave agreed.

When Vicki and Dave arrived at The Emperor, the place was filled to capacity. They sat at the bar a while before being seated. "This place is nice," Dave commented.

"Let's just hope the food is good," Vicki looked through a menu.

A waiter appeared, filling their water glasses and serving them hot tea. Vicki took a sip of the hot, soothing liquid. She rarely drank tea, but when she did it was always an enjoyable experience.

"Since we're both so hungry, how about starting off with an appetizer?" Dave suggested.

"Fine. You can do the ordering."

The waiter returned to take their order. Dave ordered a pu-pu platter followed by cashew chicken and shrimp and broccoli.

"So," Dave drawled after the waiter was gone. "How come you've been so unavailable lately?"

"I told you. I've been busy with work. It's not easy running a private practice. Until I'm earning enough to hire someone else, there are hundreds of details that have to be taken care of. Insurance forms to fill out. Statements to send. The paperwork alone takes half my time."

"You should have gone to work for a hospital like I did. There's less of that shit you have to deal with."

"We've been through this before. I want to be independent, to be my own boss. I wouldn't have that sort of control working at a hospital."

"Actually, hospitals are pretty flexible these days. Anyway, I don't want to tell you how to run your life, just this weekend. A friend of mine rented a house on the Martha's Vineyard. Have you ever been there?"

"No," Vicki admitted. She'd been all over the Cape with the exception of Martha's Vineyard.

"Well, my friend has to go out of state this weekend, meaning the house will be empty Saturday and Sunday," Dave dangled a set of keys in front of her. "Except for us."

"I can't," Vicki balked. "I have tons of paperwork I need to catch up on."

"Bring it with you. I promise I won't interfere."

"It's not even that," Vicki bit her lower lip, uncertain how to break the news.

"I'm listening," Dave folded his arms in a defensive manner.

"Pu-pu platter," the waiter announced as he placed a steaming bowl of hot appetizers in front of the pair.

"Thank you," Vicki said absently.

"Go on," Dave insisted the second the waiter was gone.

"This isn't easy for me," Vicki twisted her long blonde hair. "The truth is, I'm not really sure how I feel about you."

"What?" Dave's face turned red. "We've been sleeping together four months and now you tell me this?"

"Lower your voice," Vicki told him, as several people from nearby tables looked their way. "I'm sorry, Dave. What I need is time to decide how I feel. That's why I can't go to Martha's Vineyard with you."

"This is fucking great," Dave angrily gestured. "Here I am, stupid fool, thinking our relationship is going great and you drop this shit on me."

Vicki felt confused. What was wrong with her? Why couldn't she make it work with Dave? "I think," she began, "that it's best we remain friends for the time being. I know I made love to you earlier, but I've been meaning to talk to you about this for a long time now. I just don't know if we're right for each other, that's all."

"That's all," Dave mimicked her and threw up his hands. "You've got serious problems, Vic. I'm beginning to wonder what I ever saw in you. Now you're telling me I'm a lousy lover."

"I didn't say that," Vicki reminded him. The conversation was not going the way she wanted at all.

The waiter appeared with the Chinese dishes Dave had ordered. "Will there be anything else?" he bowed slightly.

"No," David and Vicki said together.

Dave cleared his throat. "Correct me if I'm mistaken. You're telling me you're willing to be my friend but you don't want to sleep with me anymore?"

"Just temporarily. Until I can make sense out of my feelings."

"This is fucked," Dave exclaimed. "What the hell do you expect me to do until you figure it all out? Sit on my thumbs and wait?"

"I guess," Vicki decided, "that you can date other women."

"You guess? That's mighty generous of you. You know, I should have seen all this coming between your job-related excuses and being so unavailable all the time. I intend to start dating other women. I'm only glad out relationship hadn't progressed much further or I wouldn't be taking this as well."

"I'm sorry," Vicki looked him in the eye. "I should have been honest and told you how I felt much sooner."

"Yes, you should have," Dave scolded her as they left the restaurant.

"Sorry," Vicki said again, blinking back tears. It was tough witnessing the break-up of yet another relationship. For a moment her mind flashed back to the attractive gentleman she had spilled the Pepsi on earlier in the day and she imagined having the perfect relationship with him. But he was gone and now so was Dave.

It was with a heavy heart that she went to bed with that night.

CHAPTER TWO

When the alarm clock sounded the next morning, Vicki tried her best to ignore it. But in the end its persistent buzzing won out. Reluctantly, Vicki crawled out of bed.

As she sat in her kitchen drinking coffee, her thoughts immediately focused on Dave. She was relieved that he had handled their conversation yesterday rather well. It would have made her feel worse if he hadn't. Her feelings about the whole thing were already stretched to the limit. Dave was relationship number three this year which had not worked out.

Vicki proceeded to get dressed, pondering why it was she was continually attracted to the wrong person. Actually Dave had been the best out of all the men she had dated so far. Yet that said, she could not bring herself to love him. There were too many things in his personality, which turned her off. Things like his ego, his childish mannerisms and the constant need to be the center of attention. Little things to some, but to her they took center stage. And, unfortunately for her, she had a front row seat.

When she arrived at her office, her first patient was already waiting. Stanley Minkse suffered from clinical depression.

"How are you today?" Vicki asked once they were seated.

"I'm not sure," Stanley fidgeted. It was clear he was agitated.

"You look nervous. Is the anti-depressant helping at all?"

"I don't know," Stanley ran a shaky hand through his hair. "I still feel nervous all the time."

"Is there any time during the day when you feel better?"

"No. At least, I don't think so."

For the next hour, Vicki tried to get Stanley to focus on his feelings. She reminded him that anti-depressants sometimes took weeks to work and prescribed a mild tranquilizer he could take until the medication began to work.

When he left, Vicki's thoughts once again drifted to Dave. Perhaps she had been too hasty in discontinuing the relationship. After all, he was the best of all the men she had recently dated. She should have tried harder to get over what she perceived were his faults. Given enough time the relationship might have worked. If only she wasn't such a damn perfectionist.

The ringing of the telephone startled Vicki. It was a phone call from the MMI-the Massachusetts Mental Institute—informing her that Carrie Graden had again tried to kill herself and was once more an inpatient there. Apparently Carrie had taken an overdose of Tylenol and her parents had rushed her to County Hospital's emergency room, from where she was referred to the Institute. Vicki sighed and told the psychiatrist on the other end that she would be by to see Carrie later that afternoon.

It was a nice day, so when Vicki left her office that afternoon she decided to walk to the Institute which was only thirty minutes away from downtown Boston. She bought a vanilla frozen yogurt cone from a street vendor and started on her way when she heard a voice calling her name.

"Vicki! Vic . . . Wait up!"

It was Sue, her best friend. "Susan, what are you doing in town?"

"A book I ordered from Barnes and Noble came in and I just picked it up. What are you up to? Want to go grab a bite to eat or is that ice-cream cone your dinner?"

"Actually, it's frozen yogurt and I'd love to grab a bite to eat, but later. I'm on my way to see a young patient of mine at MassMental. Want to walk with me."

"Sure. I'm not doing anything," Sue joined Vicki as they set off at a brisk pace. "So how's Dave? You two doing anything this weekend?"

"Not this weekend. Not ever."

"Huh?"

"David's gone, as in history. I let him know I needed some time to myself, that he could date other women."

"But Vic, he's such a nice guy. Any woman in her right mind would fall head over heels over him."

"Thanks."

"I'm serious. What happened?"

"Somehow it wasn't clicking between us, at least not at my end."

"Oh, Vic. You're such a perfectionist. You got to go with the flow sometimes. There is no such thing as Mr. Right. That's a myth. Dave was such a nice guy. You made such a cute couple together."

"Well, I'd rather be alone than with someone I don't like."

"You're turning thirty-nine in a few weeks. You have to find someone soon. They say if you haven't found your life partner by age forty, you probably won't."

"So? I can handle being alone. It's winding up with the wrong person that terrifies me."

"I'm not going to let up on you until you either get back together with Dave or find someone else you like. If you would like me to ask around, I will."

"NO!" Vicki shouted, nearly choking on the last bite of her frozen yogurt cone. The last thing she wanted was for Sue to be setting her up with any blind dates.

A second later MassMental came into view. It was an ulta-modern structure located just behind City Hall. Vicki and Sue approached the main desk inside and were informed Carrie was the second floor locked unit.

"This place sure is huge," Sue observed, looking around.

"It's a state hospital. Rumor has it it isn't that good either. A patient hung himself here last week despite being on a locked ward."

"That's too bad," Sue agreed. "Listen, why don't I sit here in the lobby while you go upstairs to see your patient. Try not to take too long. I'm starving."

"I'll see how it goes," Vicki took the stairs to the second floor and was buzzed into the locked unit. A nurse noted her visit and told her Carrie was in her room. With apprehension, Vicki approached that room. Inside, Carrie lay curled up on the bed, an expression of anger tensing her face.

"Carrie—it's me, Dr. Moore. May I come in?"

"Go away."

"Can I come and speak with you for a moment. I'm concerned about you."

"Like hell you are," Carrie hissed.

"Really I am," Vicki slowly entered the room. "You sound angry. Can you tell me what's making you so angry?"

"I've been seeing you three months and you don't know!"

"You haven't given me a chance to know you very well. How can I or anybody else get to know you when you refuse to let us know what's on your mind?"

"Look, I've been seeing shrinks for five years. Nothing helps. I'm sick of seeing shrinks. Now get the hell out of here!" Carrie threw her bed pillow at Vicki.

"Just because others may not have been able to help you doesn't mean you can't be helped. I'm not giving up on you, Carrie. I'm sorry you're in here. I look forward to seeing you during our regular hours when you're released."

"Whatever." Carrie turned over and completely ignored Vicki. When Vicki left the unit and went downstairs, she found Sue thumbing through an old Women's Day magazine.

"You O.K." Sue asked.

"My patient didn't exactly want to see me."

"Give it time. Sometimes it takes a while before you win someone's trust."

"I hope you're right."

"I know I am," Sue said cheerfully. "Now let's go eat!"

The following week Vicki was in her office going over some notes when the phone rang.

"Is this Dr. Moore?" the nervous caller inquired.

"Yes."

"Well…ah. This bartender I know gave me your number. He…ah…thought it might be helpful if I were to see you. I've been…well…feeling sort of depressed lately."

"Would you like to set up a consultation?" Vicki asked, reaching for her appointment book to check her schedule. Silence. The dial tone let Vicki know the caller had hung up. She stared at the phone for several seconds before placing it back in its cradle, wondering if the person she had been speaking with would call back. She went back to going over her notes and had almost forgotten about the call when an hour later the phone rang again. "Good afternoon. Dr. Moore's office."

"Hi. I spoke to you earlier. Sorry for hanging up on you like that."

"It's not a problem," Vicki assured him.

"I changed my mind," the caller explained nervously. "When could I come in for a consultation?"

Quickly Vicki thumbed through her appointment book. "I have next Thursday at three available."

"That'll be fine," the man sounded relieved.

"Can I please have your name," Vicki asked, wondering if this was Peter Jenkins friend, Lawrence Taylor.

"Lawrence Taylor," the man answered, confirming Vicki's assumption.

"I'll see you next week then," Vicki stated, but Lawrence had already hung up.

Larry Taylor paced back and forth across his spacious living room. There, I did it, he told himself. He had actually called a psychiatrist. Not that it would do any good. No one in this world could do anything regarding his problems.

However it was the nightmares which had finally pushed him over the edge. Plus all the worrying. He hadn't been spared a worry-free moment since the day he turned forty.

His turning forty was the key to all his troubles. It was at that age his father had died from a massive sudden heart attack when Lawrence was only eleven. Prior to that, his father had been in perfect health. Though it was a terrible ordeal at the time, surprisingly Larry managed to cope quite well with father's death all these years. Until now. Until he hit forty. Now every ache or pain made him nervous. Was he going to die at age forty like his father had?

Death. The word sent shivers up and down his spine. He wasn't ready to die, probably never would be. Death had caught his father unaware; he didn't want it to catch him unprepared. There had to be some meaning to life. If so, he wanted to find it. It didn't make sense. We eat, live and die. And age. That was another issue. He was so scared of getting older. Gray hairs had already appeared, sprinkled through his jet-black hair. He couldn't pull them out fast enough. He took a deep breath. Slow down. Forty isn't that old. He still had decades of life to explore.

But that's what his father had thought also. That he had all the time in the world. Death had claimed his father before he could see his only son graduate from grammar school.

He rubbed his temples. A nasty headache was beginning to form right in the back of his forehead. What if it was a brain tumor? What if he had a stroke and died right here in his living room?

SHUT UP! He mentally shouted at the part of his brain which could not stop thinking about death. What he needed was to get out for awhile, to get good and smashed. Anything to erase the death tape involuntarily playing in his head.

He grabbed his brown leather jacket and left his apartment building, walking to Faneuil Hall and planning to get drunk. If this psychiatrist couldn't help him, he felt certain he'd either wind up either like one of those drunks you see sleeping in the street or worse.

"Man, I still can't believe you broke it off with Dave," Sue groaned as she and Vicki met at Au Bon Pain for lunch. "He hasn't called you or anything, has he?"

"Nope. I hope he doesn't."

"You know, I wasn't exactly head over heels in love with Kevin when I first met him. It took months for me to realize I even liked him. Now we've been together three years and plan on getting married."

"I know," Vicki took a sip of her mocha iced coffee.

"So go on, give Dave a call. Maybe you two can still work it out somehow."

"Sue, I'm not interested in Dave. End of story."

"O.K. I can take a hint and change the subject. How's that patient doing, the one at MassMental?"

"She's still there, but should be getting out soon. It's so hard dealing with these borderline personality cases."

"How so," Sue seemed to perk up.

"Well, for one thing, they're so unpredictable and manipulative. They don't do well on any of the psyche drugs and the therapy with them is like taking a wild roller-coaster ride. One minute everything is going great, and then they go downhill and regress and you're left wondering what you did wrong."

"I see what you mean. Don't give up on this girl, whatever you do. Vic, is it O.K. if I tell you something? Something personal?

"Sure," Vicki leaned forward to hear her best friend better.

"First off, how old is your patient?"

"Nineteen."

"Well, when I was around her age, eighteen to be exact, I was diagnosed with having a borderline personality disorder."

"Really?" Vicki was amazed. "You never told me."

"That's because I consider that part of my life over and done with. I was in therapy for two years, but I did get better."

"What is it that helped you?"

"A lot of things. However, I think the diagnosis of borderline personality disorder is a catchall term. If they can't peg you into a certain category, they just say you're borderline."

"I'm sure that happens. But there are certain characteristics most borderlines share, such as self-destructive behavior or feelings of emptiness."

"What did help me was the therapy itself. Getting in touch with my feelings and stopping doing drugs."

"What kind of drugs were you on?"

"You name it, it was available at the high school I went to. I did a lot of cocaine, smoked a lot of pot. I even took acid once or twice."

"What got you to stop?"

"The therapy. My parents insisted that I go or forget all about their paying for college. I wanted to go to college really badly, so I agreed to the therapy."

"That's great," Vicki agreed. "It obviously did you some good."

"I never tried to kill myself like your patient has, but I still think once she comes to trust you and let you into her life, she'll get better.

"I hope you're right," Vicki stated with renewed optimism. If Sue could get better, maybe Carrie could too. No matter what happened from now on, she would never, ever give up on Ms. Carrie Graden.

CHAPTER THREE

For Tony Whiting, it was a terrible day all around. Hours earlier he had sold his dream—a hotel he had built from the ground up twenty years ago on what was once a seldom-used parking lot in Copley Square. It was he who had seen the potential of the land and secured the funds to build the hotel he named The Majestic. A few years later, more hotels moved into the area, the Hynes Convention Center was built and two shopping malls were added. In order to survive Tony had to expand.

Through money provided by a secret group of businessmen called The Group, Tony bought up all the remaining land surrounding his hotel for the entire block. Once the space was cleared, he immediately expanded the Majestic until it was the largest, most lavish hotel in Boston. Everyone coming to Boston wanted to stay at the Majestic. It was the best hotel around, in a class by itself. None of the smaller hotels could even begin to compete with it. The Majestic made Tony a rich, rich man.

But money wasn't everything.

If only he had let his wife Margaret drive that fateful night a year ago, then he could have gone on leading a charmed life. But no, he had to be the stubborn Scorpio. He had to insist he drive all the way from their summer home in New Hampshire back to Boston. It was a decision, which cost Margaret and their nineteen-year-old daughter Ami their lives.

He had no right to be driving, tired as he was. Three times Margaret had asked him if she could take the wheel. He said no, believing he was fine. Until he woke up at Saint Elizabeth's Hospital and learned his wife and daughter were dead. Somewhere along the road he had fallen asleep. The car veered off the road, tumbling over and over itself before coming to rest at the bottom of a steep ravine.

With all his heart, he wished that he had died that night too. The pangs of guilt were unbearable. Why, the very next day Ami had been scheduled to begin her studies at Boston Central University. Now she was buried beneath the cold ground at the Forest Hills Cemetery. So was Margaret. Poor, sweet Margaret. If only he had listened to her and allowed her to take the wheel that night, none of this would ever have happened. Words could never adequately describe how much much he missed his wife.

Life for Tony lost all of its meaning following the accident. He found himself consumed by depression and rage. Even the Majestic, once his source of pride and accomplishment, no longer gave him joy. Why should he bother with something that no longer brought him happiness? He had all the money he'd ever need. So he decided to sell the Majestic, on this his forty-ninth birthday.

"What are you doing tonight?" Sandy Rosen inquired.

"I have a date with Alfred. You know, the guy who's into garter-belts," Kim Long responded.

"He's such a cheapskate! How'd you like to make some real money tonight?"

"I'm listening," Kim became interested.

"I just got off the phone with Shawna," Sandy explained. "She called to ask whether we'd be available to work a party tonight. I told her yes. We're supposed to meet her downstairs in an hour."

"You told her yes without checking with me first?"

"I didn't think you'd mind, especially when you find out how much money is involved."

Kim raised an eyebrow. "How much money are we talking about here?"

"Brace yourself," Sandy advised with a grin. "Are you ready?"

Kim nodded.

"Two thousand dollars apiece!"

"Two thousand dollars!" Kim nearly fell off the chair she was sitting on. The lipstick she had been putting on fell out of her hand.

"Tell me it ain't worth canceling your date with Alfred for that kind of money?"

"Wait a minute," suspicion crept into Kim's voice. "Exactly what kind of party is this that they're willing to pay us that kind of money? It better not be anything too weird or kinky."

Sandy shook her head. "It's nothing like that. Shawna gave me her word. It's just some birthday party for some big shot. All we're supposed to do is service the birthday boy and the other men that'll be there. Shawna thinks we might make at least a grand in tips on top of the two we're getting paid."

"Wow. How'd she hook into a deal like this?"

"She's been around a lot longer than us. She's gotta be at least thirty now. Anyway, she has this rich sugar daddy named Dick who asked her and two other pros to do the party."

"I wish I had a sugar daddy," Kim mused. "I'm lucky if I can squeeze out a fifty from Alfred or any other of my tricks."

"Same here," Sandy sighed. "But remember. We're only nineteen and Shawna's like thirty. She's been around the block a few times. Sooner or later, we'll probably nail a live one too."

"Let's hope," Kim resumed applying her red lipstick. "Do you ever—you know—regret getting into the life?"

"Sometimes. But I look at it this way. I had no choice. Did you?"

"No," Kim whispered.

"One day we'll hit it big, you'll see. Then we can move out of this dump and let the cockroaches have the whole place."

Kim laughed. "So what are you going to wear tonight?"

"My red top and mini-dress. What about you?"

Kim scanned her closet and chose a revealing white blouse to go with her bright pink shorts. A pair of large hoop earrings and black spike heels made her look just like the stereotypical hooker. So did the blue eye shadow and gleaming red lipstick. Her long, black hair hung loosely to her waist.

"You look good," Shawna complimented Kim. "If I were a guy, I'd be all over you."

"Thanks," Kim laughed. "You don't look so bad yourself."

"Let's go make some money," Sandy shouted as both girls left the apartment.

Angel went from woman to woman faster than a bee gathered nectar from flower to flower. He discovered that women were divided into two camps: ones who liked him and ones who did not. The ones who didn't like him he didn't worry about. The ones who liked him he used for all they were worth. After all, that's what he felt the woman who liked him were for. Personally put on this earth to please him.

It helped if they had money. A lot of money. If money were nowhere to be found, neither was Angel. What he lacked in looks he made up for in expensive clothes, motorcycles and drugs. Though his drug of choice was cocaine, he could use and get anything else the streets had to offer.

During the day he worked construction, a job he hated. He was just about to quit that miserable trade. All he needed was some vulnerable woman to take him in and support him. He thought he had found just such a person in Sandy Rosen.

Ah, Sandy. She was one of those women who really liked him. Too bad he didn't feel the same way. To him, Sandy was like a rag, someone he'd use prior to discarding. Which might be a while, since Sandy's prostitution provided a steady income. It was lucky for him he had met her through a mutual friend that frequented Boston's Combat Zone.

It was Sandy's roommate Kim whom Angel was initially interested in, but the bitch would have nothing to do with him. So he had to settle for Sandy, a lesser conquest in every way. Still, the second he abandoned his job, he felt completely secure that Sandy was wrapped enough around his finger to support him.

He parked his Harley-Davidson on Washington Street, looking up and down the street to see if Sandy was around. It was certainly late enough for her to be working the street. Conveniently the apartment Sandy shared with Kim was located right smack in the middle of the Zone on Washington Street. It was situated over an adult bookstore. While Angel would have preferred living somewhere else, he could make due living in the heart of the Zone until a better arrangement came along. One good thing about it was that he'd be close to his drug connection, who worked out of the very bookstore Angel would soon be living above.

Angel grinned and hopped off his motorcycle. There was Sandy standing near the adult bookstore with Kim and another hooker named Shawna. Sandy spotted him and waved, all smiles to see him. He strode over to the girls. "Hi Sweets," he gave Sandy a passionate kiss on the lips. "Evenin' ladies," he addressed Shawna and Kim who scarcely paid him notice. He put his arm around Sandy, hugging her close. "Do you love me?"

"More than anything," Sandy giggled.

"Good." It was exactly what Angel wanted to hear.

A silver Cadillac turned onto Washington Street from Stuart. "There's Dick," Shawna waved so he would see them.

"I gotta go," Sandy told Angel. "I'll see you tomorrow."

"You bet."

Dick pulled up to the curb and the girls climbed into the vehicle. "I love you," Sandy blew Angel a kiss out the window before the car pulled away.

Yes, Angel smiled. He had Sandy right where he wanted her.

Shawna was sitting in the front seat with Dick. She slid over and gave him a kiss. "How are you doing?"

"Great. Glad to see you. Who'd you bring?"

"Sandy and Kim. That's Sandy in the red skirt and Kim in the pink shorts."

"Do the two of you know what kind of party you'll be working?"

"Shawna said it was a birthday party for some big shot," Sandy exclaimed.

Dick smiled. "You're quite right. It's a very special birthday for a good friend of mine. Do you know who Tony Whiting is?"

"I don't think so," Sandy told him.

"Wait a minute. I know," Kim said. "He owns the Majestic, right?"

"Used to own the Majestic. Today he sold it, so he's feeling kind of down. I want you girls to do everything you can to cheer him up, understand?"

"Sure thing," Sandy stated and Kim nodded her agreement.

"My friend is rather depressed because of this being his birthday and him selling the hotel," Dick explained. "Around a year ago he lost his wife and daughter in a car crash he blames himself for. In fact, his daughter Ami looked like you Kim."

"Really?"

"On his way back from his summer place in New Hampshire, Tony fell asleep at the wheel and his car plummeted down a steep ravine near Braintree. His wife died on the spot, Ami a few hours later."

"That's terrible," Kim shuddered.

"The guilt devastated Tony," Dick continued. "Overnight he became a different person."

"I can imagine." Sandy said.

"That's why Dick wants this party to be special," Shawna explained to her friends. "Now that Tony's sold the Majestic, there's nothing in his life.

"Frankly, I'm worried about him," Dick made known. "Over the last year other than on business, he hasn't socialized with any of his friends. He's hardly even looked at another woman. This party's being held at my place in Dover. It took a lot of convincing to get him out here. Most other times he refused. When he found out this was a birthday party for him, he couldn't say no this time. He has no idea I asked you three girls to take care of us men there tonight. Tony's never had a pro before, so he might be a little nervous. When we get to my place, I'll send you three up to my bedroom, where I told Tony to wait until I got back. See how it goes. If he wants only one girl, let him decide whom. After you're finished with him, there are scores of other men who'll be lining up for your services. Before you leave, see me and I'll make sure you are paid. Of course all of you can keep any tips you make."

"Sounds like my kind of party!" Kim exclaimed happily. She could sense this was going to be the best night of her life.

Tony Whiting sat on the edge of a king-size waterbed in Dick's spacious upstairs bedroom. Downstairs he could hear the sounds of a party in full swing, but he was in no mood to party.

In fact, just being in Dick's bedroom was bothering him. Dick had said he'd be right up with a birthday present. That was half an hour ago. Dick's bedroom was designed solely for sex and it made Tony uncomfortable. The most noticeable feature was the overhead mirror. It had startled him when he first looked up. Whatever was the present Dick had for him, he hoped to get it soon so he could go home. In the midst of all his personal problems, socializing with other members of The Group was not a priority.

There was another condition bothering Tony following the accident and his own guilt in causing it. Once when he was at the doctor's he came close to blurting it out but stopped himself. It was too embarrassing. He was impotent. Truth was, he had no interest in sex anymore. That's why being in Dick's bedroom made him so nervous. He was just about to get up off the bed and head downstairs when the door knob began to turn. Dick must have come back.

"Surprise," Shawna, Kim and Sandy entered, singing a cheerful rendition of 'Happy Birthday.'

His face turned ash white. How stupid! He should have known why Dick put him in the bedroom. What the hell was he going to do with three girls?

Suddenly he blinked, not believing his eyes. Ami! His dead daughter had come back from the dead to him!

Of course Tony knew it wasn't so, couldn't be so. Yet the resemblance was absolutely striking. "You," he pointed a trembling finger at Kim. "Come over here."

Kim stood in front of Tony.

It was amazing. The girl standing in front of him resembled Ami in every way. The long, silky black hair, the green eyes . . . there wasn't anybody who could have told him this wasn't Ami. He couldn't take his eyes off her. "What's your name?"

"Kimberly. But everyone calls me Kim."

The voice! Even the voice was that of Ami!

"How old are you, Kim?"

"Nineteen."

She was Ami's age too!

"I'm Shawna and this is Sandy," Shawna spoke up.

But Tony didn't even notice them. He kept staring at Kim and seemed to be mumbling something to himself.

Not knowing what to do, Kim suggestively placed her hand on his thigh.

Tony jumped back as though burned by fire. "What are you doing?"

It was not the reaction Kim hoped for. She hoped this trick didn't turn out to be one of the difficult ones. "I thought you might want to have a little fun."

"Why don't Sandy and I leave," Shawna suggested. "That way you could be alone with Kim."

Tony nodded and the two girls departed.

Kim began to take off her top. When she was naked she sat at the edge of the bed and began to undo Tony's tie.

"I can't do this," Tony jumped back.

"Don't I turn you on," Kim asked.

"No!"

"No!" Kim was insulted. She began to put her clothes back on. No man had ever suggested she was unattractive.

"Wait," Tony said as Kim headed towards the door.

"What for?" Kim demanded. "You don't seem to like me much."

"That's the problem. I like you too much."

"Huh?"

"You see, you look just like the daughter I had but lost."

Vaguely Kim remembered Dick saying something to that effect. "If you like, I can ask Sandy or Shawna to come up. That way you won't feel like you're having sex with your dead daughter."

"I'm not interested in having sex. I'm interested in you. How did you get started in this life?"

"It's a long story."

"Will you tell me about it someday?"

"I thought you weren't interested in me."

"No. Not sexually. Kim, I'm a rich man with no one to spend my money on. Why don't you let me help you? Why don't you let me take you out of having to hustle for a living?"

"What do you have in mind?" This just might end up working to her advantage. She could be staring at what was the ultimate aim in her prostitution: a rich sugar daddy to take care of all her needs.

"I'd like to get to know you much better, Kim. Find out what your dreams are, what your desires are. You're so much like my daughter I can't believe it. There wasn't anything I wouldn't do for Ami. You could fill an empty hole in my life, Kim. I'll give you my phone number. Promise you'll call me and come to my penthouse suite at the Prudential Towers to talk. Promise me."

"I promise," Kim said, wondering what Tony had in mind for her.

CHAPTER FOUR

Never did Lawrence Taylor feel more nervous in his life. His making an appointment to see a shrink was a mistake. A big, fat, stupid, asinine mistake. It was hard for him to talk about personal things that mattered to him. He felt ashamed of losing control over a significant portion of his life.

The elevator doors opened and unsteadily Larry got off of it. He did not want to be here. Instantly he spotted the sign on the door. VICTORIA. B. MOORE—PSYCHIATRY it read. It was enough to send him into a panic.

It's not too late, he reminded himself. He didn't have to go through with it. Escape was but an elevator's ride away. No one would know how close he had actually come to seeing a shrink. He stood by the door trying to decide if he should enter. Then, slowly, his hand reached for the doorknob. It was now or never.

Lawrence eased the door open and found himself standing in a small, comfortable waiting room. Anxiously, he sat down in one of the chairs. It still wasn't too late. He could still rush out and the psychiatrist would never know he had even showed for his appointment. In an effort to distract himself, he began to thumb through an old TIME magazine. If this psychiatrist didn't show up soon, he was certain he was going to jump out of his skin.

Vicki sat in her office going over some articles she had researched on borderline personality disorder. It was fascinating reading, but she had heard her three o'clock client enter, so she gathered her papers up and placed them on a shelf. It was time to greet her new patient.

The door from the inner office opened and Larry jumped out of his seat. It looked like he was destined to go through a psychiatric session after all.

Vicki looked at the nervous-looking client standing there and nearly collapsed. It was the Pepsi guy! Her new client, Lawrence Taylor, was none other then the handsome stranger she had spilled Pepsi on the day she had rushed out of the Baker's Shoe Store. "Good afternoon," her voice trembled slightly. "I'm Dr. Victoria Moore. You must be Lawrence Taylor."

"Do I know you from somewhere?"

"Possibly you've seen me around town. Won't you come into my office?"

Larry snapped his fingers. "That's it! You're the lady who spilled that can of Pepsi on me recently. Remember?"

"Vaguely," Vicki mumbled. Lawrence was even more handsome than she remembered.

Larry sat down in one of the comfortable leather chairs in her office and tried to relax.

"Can you tell me a little of why you're here?" Vicki sat down opposite him, noticing his tension.

"I still can't believe that you're my shrink," Larry shook his head at the strange turn of events.

"Do you have a problem with that?"

"No."

"Neither do I." She was just going to have to keep any attraction she felt for Larry under wraps. "Now, over the telephone you indicated that you were depressed. What makes you think so?"

"It's the way I'm feeling lately. I'm not getting any sleep. I guess that's my main complaint. Every night I wake up from some sort of nightmare."

"Do you remember any of them?"

"Yes," Larry shuddered. He hated to even talk about them. "Well, in some, I'm attacked by a wild animal or person, mutilated into dozens of pieces. Sometimes I dream I'm tied to a stake and set on fire. These nightmares seem so real when I'm having them. I even had one where I dreamed a big shark was eating me alive. There's one common theme in all of them, though. Without fail, in every single scenario, I die."

"I see," Vicki jotted this fact down. "Is death something you often think about?"

"Lately, yes."

"Why do you suppose that is?"

"It all started when I turned forty."

"What happened when you turned forty?"

"I know this is going to sound irrational, but my dad died at forty from a sudden heart attack. The man was in perfect health the day he dropped dead. He exercised, didn't smoke or drink, and he watched what he ate. He came home from work and was just about to sit down to supper, when he grabbed his chest and collapsed."

"How old were you at the time?"

"Eleven. I ran out of the house screaming. My mom called for an ambulance and left me with some neighbors when it came. When she came back from the hospital, she confirmed what I suspected. That he was dead."

"How did you cope with the news?"

"Terrible. My mom told me I needed to be strong, that I was now the man of the house, and somehow I pulled through. For a long time, I didn't even think about my dad all that much. This turning forty really has me scared though. I feel like I'm going to die too. Every ache, every pain, I'm certain is from some disease and I'm going to croak."

"Now, have you been examined by a medical doctor," Vicki paused to ask.

"Yes, I have been, and according to him, I'm in perfect health," Larry laughed. "It's crazy, right? For me to be in perfect health and still feel this way."

"I think you have a lot of issues around your dad's death and the fact that you're growing older. Are you employed."

"I work at the Ideal Advertising Agency."

"What do you do there?"

"A little of everything. Basically, I work with Mr. Josh Hillman on client accounts and advertising strategies."

"Are you happy with your job?"

"I can't complain. It was my first job offer when I graduated from Harvard Business School and I make a good salary."

"Have you ever been married?"

"No."

"Are you in a serious relationship?" Deep down, Vicki hoped he would say no.

"No."

"How do you spend your time when you're not working?"

"I'm miserable when I'm not working. Work distracts me from myself. I have this friend, Bob, who I used to party with. He calls me to go out with him and have a good time. I don't know. I've seemed to have outgrown that. Lately I just want to be by myself."

"Do you take any medications?"

"No. Just an occasional aspirin. I often wake up from these nightmares with a severe headache."

"Are you using and drugs or alcohol?"

"I haven't used any drugs since my teens, but I am drinking a lot more recently to try to get me to sleep," Larry explained.

"If I asked you to stop drinking while we continue to meet on a weekly basis, would that be a problem?"

"No, I don't think so."

"Good. I think I have all the information I need for now. With your permission, we'll meet each Thursday at three. I want you to stop drinking, and for a few nights I'm going to give you a mild tranquilizer to help you sleep. After that, I want you to try some more natural approaches, such as taking hot baths or working out before bed. The alcohol might have helped in the short run, but it can only cause more problems if you continue to abuse it. I think with you coming here and talking about your anxieties, we'll get to the bottom of your depression."

"So you think I can get better?" Larry asked hopefully.

"I think we can examine your life and bring you some relief," Vicki stated before ending their session.

Larry struggled with his thoughts as he waited for the elevator following his therapy hour. He really liked his psychiatrist and decided he wanted to work with her in getting to know himself better. It was weird to be talking about his thoughts on death and dying when his natural urge was to suppress his feelings. Usually by drinking.

Drinking. That's what he felt like doing right now. But Dr. Moore had told him to stop drinking. Oh well, he could still go to a bar and sip soda water. The elevator doors opened and Larry took it to the lobby. He walked through downtown Boston and headed to Faneuil Hall, taking in the sights and sounds as other people bustled about with purpose. Ultimately, he wound up at Snifters, a bar popular with the Yuppie crowd.

"Good evening, Mr. Taylor," a bartender whom had come to know Larry from previous visits greeted him. "What'll it be today? A highball? A black Russian?"

"Just a soda water, Ed," Larry said, taking off his leather jacket and seating himself at the bar.

"That's a good one," Ed laughed. "Seriously, what can I get you?"

"I'm serious. I'm trying to cut down some."

"One soda water, coming up. I'm glad you're cutting back some. The way you were drinking last time you were here made me wonder if you were trying to drink yourself to death."

Larry cringed at Ed's choice of words. Just the mention of the word death was enough to jump-start his preoccupation with it.

"What's the matter? Did I say something wrong? Your smile just turned upside down."

"It's nothing. Don't worry about it," Larry unfurled a straw and stuck it in his soda water. He took a sip. No question about it: beer was better.

Three hours and five soda waters later, Larry got up to leave the bar and put on his jacket.

"Leaving so soon?" Ed teased. "Have another soda water. On the house."

"No, it's O.K." Larry answered. "I couldn't deal with another glass of the stuff. Besides, I've been here long enough. What I need to do is go home and try to get some sleep."

"Having trouble getting to sleep lately?"

"Pretty much."

"I can relate," Ed yawned. "Gotta be the weather."

"Maybe," Larry said, not wishing to get into it. The night felt cool and crisp as he exited Snifters. Leisurely Larry strolled through Faneuil Hall. A magician was performing on the front steps of Quincy Market and he slowed down to watch. First the magician held out a long piece of rope and instructed someone from the crowd to cut the rope into three pieces. When the rope was cut, the man held out a paper bad so the audience could see it was empty. He put the pieces of rope inside the bag and closed it. Then he chanted a few magical phrases. Presto! When he opened the bag the rope he removed was once again long and solid. People began to clap and drop dollar bills into a plastic bucket being passed around.

Larry dropped a dollar into the bucket and left. He was feeling tired. Whether or not he got any sleep was a different story, but now would be good time to try. Fortunately, the apartment building where he lived was only fifteen minutes away. Stifling a yawn, he took off walking down Devonshire Street, which would take him to his building. Compared to Faneuil Hall, Devonshire Street was a ghost town. Every now and then he would come across a homeless person sleeping in one of the alleys, but that was about it.

When Larry arrived home, he quickly took a hot shower and popped one of the Dalmane the doctor had prescribed. Twenty minutes later, he drifted off into a deep, mostly trouble-free, sleep.

"I agree Ms. Graden suffers from borderline personality disorder," declared Dr. Marshall Peters to Vicki. They were sitting in his office at MassMental going over Carrie's file. "I think it might be helpful if you were to see Ms. Graden more often, say, three times a week instead of two."

"I'd be glad to."

"I also recommended several day treatment programs to the family. They expressed an interest and would like to consult with you about that."

"I'd like to work with them on how to best help Carrie. I'm hoping she can get better."

"Good. Sometimes these borderline patients can be helped, sometimes they can't. I'm sure you'll do your best. Thank you for coming in. I'll be discharging Ms. Graden in a few days. Call me if I can offer any further assistance."

"Thank you," Vicki said, leaving his office. She boarded a trolley at Haymarket Station to go downtown, thinking it would be faster that walking. No such luck. The trolley grunted to a complete stop between Government Center and Park Street, and the lights went off.

"Ladies and gentlemen, we apologize for the inconvenience," the car's speakers boomed as people groaned. "We should be moving momentarily."

Vicki glanced at her watch. She was going to be late for her second session with Mr. Taylor! She looked forward to seeing him again.

Twenty minutes later, the trolley roared to life and she arrived safely at Park Street.

Larry was sitting in the waiting area when she made it to her office. "Sorry I'm late," she exclaimed. "Let's go into my office," she led the way and the two took their usual seats.

"Why were you late?" Larry asked.

"How do you feel about me being late?" Vicki turned the question around.

"Well, I figure since I'm paying for the full hour, I should get it."

"Do you feel angry that I'm late? Disappointed?"

"Disappointed, maybe. I had hoped you cared enough about me to at least be on time for my session."

"Perhaps you feel if your father had cared enough about you, he might not have died."

"This has nothing to do with my dad," Larry firmly stated.

"I think it does."

"Whatever."

"Tell me about your dad? Were you close to him? Did you do things together?"

"He worked a lot. He was a manager at the Keystone factory. They produced automotive parts. But, yeah. We were close. He used to take me fishing over the weekends. Or bowling. Or to the movies. He always had time for me."

"Do you have any brothers or sisters?"

"No. I was an only child."

"What was your mother like? Is she still alive?"

"She lives in a one-family house in East Boston. I visit her often. She means the world to me."

"How do you get along?"

"Great. I love her more than anything."

"How have the nightmares been since I last saw you?"

"I actually had a couple of good nights."

"So the nightmares are diminishing?"

"Somewhat."

"Are you still thinking a lot about death and dying."

"Yes. I'm really afraid. I'm so scared of dying like you wouldn't believe."

"What do you think happens when you die?"

"Nothingness. We return to nothingness."

"That frightens you?"

"Yes."

"You're scared of letting go of this life?"

"Yes. It'll be like a giant eraser has erased me."

"You'd lose all awareness."

"I know. I guess you can't help me after all. You can't make me live forever."

"Nothing or no one can make you live forever. But our work together can make you live more comfortably for the years you have ahead of you."

"I guess I'll have to settle for that, then," Larry reasoned, opening up to Vicki for the remainder of the session. He told her all about his life, beginning with his childhood to his current job at Ideal Advertising. They discussed his personal feelings and dreams he had for his life. When the hour was over for Larry, it felt like a huge weight had been lifted from his shoulders.

The following week, both Larry and Vicki were on time.

"How are you doing?" Vicki asked Larry.

"I haven't had any nightmares since our last session. That alone is an improvement."

"I think it is. I think us examining your life and finding more healthful ways for you to cope is helping. Have you stopped drinking?"

"Haven't had a drop in two weeks now."

"Good. I can tell you're trying really hard to beat this depression."

"You know, now that I've had time to think about it, I've probably been depressed for a long time. It just came to a head when I turned forty."

"I think you're right. Usually depression takes a long time to build. The shock of your father's death might have set it off and it continued to build from there."

"All that partying I did for all those years may have been just to fill the emptiness inside of me."

"Could be. Tell me about the emptiness."

"It's like a black void, from which nothing escapes. There is no bottom to it, only nothingness. Like a black hole."

"Last week you mentioned that was similar to your thoughts on what death would be like. It's almost like you feel like you're dying when you're very much alive."

"What can fill this void? I feel so empty."

"Again, that's what our work here will seek to do. The more you know yourself, the less empty you should feel. Last week you really opened up and came to grips with feelings you've suppressed for years. I think the more you do that, the better you'll feel."

"I'm scared you'll abandon me during the process," Larry revealed.

"Of course, like your father abandoned you by dying when you really needed him in your life."

"I can see the connection."

"I'll do my best to be there for you," Vicki promised. Any attraction she felt for Lawrence, well, she'd just have to deal with it.

CHAPTER FIVE

Try as he would, Tony Whiting could not get Kim long out off his mind. He almost felt like searching for her. She had triggered so many memories of his dead daughter, Ami. It was incredible two people could look so much alike. He felt really bad for her, so young and involved in a life of prostitution. What kind of life could she have had? He was ready to take her out of it, if only she'd let him.

The phone rang, and Tony jumped up from his sofa. What if it was Kim? She had promised him she'd call. "Hello," he said eagerly.

"Hello, Tony?"

"Yes."

"It's me, Kim. We met at a party a few days ago, and you asked me to call you. Remember?"

How could he forget! "Of course I remember. I was sitting here hoping you'd call."

"You suggested we get together to talk. Do you still want to? I can be there in a little while."

"I live at the penthouse suite of the North Prudential Tower. Do you know where that is?"

It was one of the most sought after addresses in Boston. Of course Kim knew where it was. "I can be there in thirty minutes."

"I'll be waiting," Tony told her.

"Hold your horses," Angel shouted behind the closed bathroom door.

"Hurry the hell up," Kim pounded on the door. "I need to use the mirror." She wanted her make-up to be perfect when she went to see Tony. This could be her chance to score a rich sugar daddy.

Now Angel was tying up the bathroom. A week ago he had moved into the apartment she shared with Sandy and he was making her life miserable. Whatever did her roommate see in him? As soon as she could, she wanted to move out of the apartment. Perhaps Tony would help her.

"Hurry up," Kim banged on the door. She resumed pounding on it until Angel finally came out.

"What's your hurry?" Angel smirked. "Can't a guy take a shit in peace in this place?"

Kim ignored him and proceeded to get ready. When she was sure her make-up was perfect, she ran downstairs and hailed a cab.

"Where to?" a cigar-smoking cabbie grumbled.

"The Prudential Towers," Kim told him, feeling like a big shot in giving him this address.

She was nervous as she entered the lobby of the north Tower. It was impressive. Oriental carpeting, leather furniture and polished brass trim everywhere. A heavy, ornate chandelier swayed from the ceiling.

"Can I help you, miss," a security guard seated behind a massive oak desk asked her.

"I'm here to visit Mr. Whiting."

"What is your name?"

"Kim. He's expecting me."

"There's a young lady named Kim to see you, sir," the guard spoke into an intercom.

"Send her up," Kim could hear Tony say.

The guard pushed a leather-bound book towards her. "If you'd be kind enough to sign your full name in this book for our records, you can go on up."

With a shaky scrawl, Kim signed her name and got on the elevator to take her to the penthouse.

"It's great to see you!" Tony greeted Kim when she arrived at his suite. He had come so close to calling her Ami just now.

"I'm glad to see you, too."

"I've thought a lot about you since the party," Tony admitted. "Come on in. Let me show you how I live."

The apartment was modern, luxurious. A Baby Grand piano took center stage in the living room. "Do you play?" Kim asked.

"My wife used to," Tony answered sadly.

Tony showed her the rest of his apartment, including the sauna and hot tub in the bathroom. Then he motioned for Kim to sit down beside him on his white leather sofa. He picked up a photo album from the coffee table and flipped through its pages, taking one out and passing it to Kim.

For a minute Kim stared at the photo. It was of a young girl standing beside a boat. The girl looked exactly like her. "This is a picture of your daughter, isn't it?" Kim gasped. "God, she looks just like me."

Tony nodded. "Exactly like you."

"What was her name?"

"Ami."

"That's a pretty name."

"It's because of me that she's dead. Did you know that?" The pain was evident in Tony's voice.

"Dick vaguely told us about some accident while we were on the way to the party."

"I fell asleep at the wheel and lost control of my car. My wife died on the spot, Ami a few hours later. I've never forgiven myself."

"You can't blame yourself. You had no way of knowing an accident would happen."

"I should have known. I was sleepy and should never have been at the wheel. Do you know, you're the first person I've had up here since the accident? Or that Ami was about to become a freshman at Boston Central University right before she died?"

"You said you wanted to help me. How?" Kim wondered. It was all interesting how she resembled Ami, but it was time to start talking money. She desperately wanted, no, needed, to get out of the apartment she now shared with Sandy and Angel.

"Perhaps you'll think I'm crazy, but I want to help you leave the life. Do you have a high school diploma?"

"I do, but what's that got to do with anything?"

"Well, I was thinking, wouldn't it be great if you were to go to Boston Central in Ami's place? Ami's gone. I can't help her anymore. But I'd like to help you. I have all sorts of connections and could get you in for the September semester of this year. I'll pay for everything. Dorm room, meals, books, everything."

Never before had Kim even considered college. Tony's suggestion was something she never expected. Still, what did she have to lose? She'd be out of the apartment and Angel would be out of her life. She wouldn't have to bother squeezing money out of tricks like Alfred anymore. The idea intrigued her. Kimberly Long—College Student. "I'll have to think about it," she finally told Tony.

"That's all I can ask."

"I'm not Ami and can't pretend to be her."

"I'm not asking you to. No one could ever take Ami's place. Yet you look so much like her that I want to help you. Consider me a crazy man trying to relieve some of my guilt. My offer to you is sincere. Promise me you'll seriously consider it. Surely, you can't be enjoying what you do now?"

Kim bit her lip. "Some of the time I enjoy it."

"A girl your age should be thinking of school and her future, not frolicking in the sack with dirty old men. Tell me, how did you get into hooking?"

"When my mom died, I was seventeen. My dad was always molesting me, but with her gone, it got even worse. One day, he finally did it. He crawled into my bed and raped me. I ran away the next day. I soon found I needed money to survive, that I couldn't be sleeping in the Common or begging for very long. Winter was coming. One day, while I was begging for some change, some guy offered me thirty bucks for a quick blow job. I was scared, but I went with him to his car. Five minutes later, I was thirty bucks richer. I knew the Combat Zone had a lot of hookers, so I headed there and have turned tricks since then. It wasn't great, but it sure beat freezing my ass off on street corners off for a few measly pennies."

Tony was shocked. "Have you seen your father since he raped you?"

"No," Kim shook her head. "As far as I'm concerned, I've erased the name Clark Long from my mind."

"It must be difficult for you to be out on your own, without no one to turn to?"

She shrugged, trying not to let her feelings show. "Those are the breaks. Life isn't fair. Some of us make out better that others. I've had Sandy and Shawna to turn to before. I'm hoping now I have you."

Tony put his arm around Kim. "I want you to be one of those people who make out well in life, Kim. You're not alone anymore. Five years from now you could be a college graduate and all this could be nothing but an unpleasant memory. It'll ease some of my guilt but also you'll benefit by turning your life around and living up to your full potential. Promise me you'll think seriously about my offer and get back to me tomorrow. In the meantime, I'll give you a thousand dollars. That and what you made at the party should last you a while so you wouldn't need to turn any tricks. As soon as you decide what to do, call me. Call me tomorrow. I'm here for you."

Had he done enough to persuade her? Tony wondered for a long time after Kim left. This idea of helping someone had renewed a sense of purpose to his life. Kim was such an intelligent woman and he felt she'd be successful in any endeavor. However, one thing about their conversation bothered him so much he decided to take action. He'd do anything for Kim, now or always. He picked up the phone and called a member of The Group. If anyone could exact revenge on Clark Long for what he did to Kim, The Group could.

Clark Long was very excited, downright giddy. Things were finally going swell with Lily, his new next door neighbor. In fact, she had invited him over for dinner again tonight. Lily was nice, but who Clark really had his sights on was Lily's six-year-old daughter, Tessa.

Tessa was the sweetest, most beautiful little girl he had ever seen. Other than Kim, of course. He often wondered what happened to his daughter after her rape, but he didn't waste time contemplating Kim's fate for too long. There were too many younger, highly attractive girls out there for his pleasure. Tessa, for instance.

Clark popped a mint into his mouth and rang the bell to Lily's house.

"Who is it?" he could hear Tessa's sweet little voice call.

"It's me, Clark. Your next door neighbor."

"Oh," Tessa exclaimed, opening the door.

"Hi. Is your mother at home?" Just looking at Tessa was making him hot. Why'd she have to have such deep chestnut brown eyes and fine curly blonde hair?

"Ma," Tessa called. "It's that guy again."

"Hello," Lily said, coming out of the kitchen. She was wiping her hands on a dishtowel. "I'm glad you could make it."

"My pleasure," Clark told her, planting a kiss on her left cheek. "These are for you."

"Roses. How beautiful! Tessa, look at the yellow roses. Why don't you go put them in some water for mommy?"

"O.K." Tessa said, running up and taking the bouquet from her mother.

"I hope you like roast beef," Lily asked Clark as the walked into the kitchen.

"Love it," he assured her. He took a seat at the kitchen table. "Can I help with anything?"

"I've got it all under control," Lily told him, placing a platter loaded with roast beef on the table. Next she brought out bowls of mashed potatoes and sliced carrots. "Tessa! It's dinner time!"

Tessa ran up to the table clutching a Barbie doll in her hand. "This is my new doll, Mr. Long," she gushed, showing the doll to Clark.

"I'm sure Mr. Long doesn't want to look at Barbie dolls," Lily smiled.

"No. I do. Really," Clark corrected Lily. Part of his strategy was to make Tessa like him and gain her trust. "What's her name, sweetheart?" he asked.

"Linda. I named her after my best friend in the whole wide world," Tessa beamed.

"That was very thoughtful of you," Clark managed a crooked smile.

"I know," Tessa agreed, sitting down at the table. That's when she noticed them. "Mom, I hate carrots," she whined.

"Honey, you've got to eat at least some of them," Lily said wearily. "They're good for you."

"Your mother's right," Clark agreed. "You should eat at least some of them."

Lily ate her meal in silence, observing Clark. All these years of being a single mother were taking their toll on her. She felt really fortunate a man like Clark was taking an interest in her situation. Besides, Tessa seemed to like him and that to her was the most important consideration.

"Thanks for a delicious meal," Clark said when they finished eating. "Let me help you clean up a bit here," he offered. Lily protested, but Clark insisted. Together they cleared the table and washed the dishes.

"I have a favor to ask you," Lily began as they enjoyed some after-dinner coffee later.

"Ask me anything," Clark dared without any hesitation.

"It's my job," Lily sighed. "They want me to go to Seattle this weekend for a conference. I'd really rather not take Tessa. So, if it absolutely presents no problem for you, I was wondering, well, if you'd be willing to take her. It'd only be for three days."

"Say no more," Clark interjected. "Consider it done."

"Really?"

"I'd be glad to watch her this weekend. Tessa and I are buddies."

Lily gave Clark an impulsive hug. "Thank you. Being new to this neighborhood, I really have no one else to ask. I'm so grateful you agreed. It's a relief knowing Tessa will be staying with someone I trust."

"I'll take excellent care of her," Clark promised. He couldn't envision a better situation. Now he could really have some fun with Tessa.

"I know you will," Lily smiled. "In fact, I appreciate all the attention you've given us since we moved here. It's been nice cooking for you and having you over so often. I never thought I'd meet another man I liked so much."

"It's been great for me too. I've enjoyed your company and Tessa is such a precious child."

"She is, isn't she," Lily beamed. She felt so natural with Clark, so relaxed. Just then the phone rang. "Now who can that be?" Lily wondered. "Excuse me."

"I think I'll go in the living room and see what Tessa's up to while you're on the phone," Clark decided. He strode into the room. Tessa was sitting on the floor surrounded by a circle of Barbie dolls. "That's a lot of dolls," he sat down on the carpet beside her.

"You can never have enough Barbies," Tessa said matter-of-factly.

"That's true," Clark agreed. "While your mom's sway this weekend, let's say I take you shopping? I'll buy you all the Barbies you want."

"Wow!" Tessa gave Clark a quick hug. "Thank you."

Clark checked to hear if Lily was still on the phone. She was. He hugged Tessa back, sticking his hand under her dress.

Not even knowing what he was doing, the girl instinctively pulled away.

"Yes sir," Clark whispered. "We're going to have a lot of fun with this weekend. "Boy, can my sister ever talk," Lily breezed into the room. "Sorry for taking so long."

"Tessa and I were just playing with her Barbie dolls. She has quite a collection here."

"I confess. I spoil her."

"I hope you won't get mad, but I promised Tessa I'd take her shopping for more dolls while you're in Seattle."

"You shouldn't have," Lily now hugged him. "You're too thoughtful as it is."

"I should get going," Clark said, getting up from the floor.

"Someday we have to get together, just you and I," Lily cooed.

"I'd like that," Clark lied. Lily didn't excite him at all. Tessa did. But if he had to woo Lily to get to Tessa, so be it. Besides, he was going to be all alone with Tessa for three whole days.

"I'll drop Tessa by Friday afternoon."

"Perfect," he gave Lily a kiss and began to walk to his house. Funny, the lights were on in his house. He didn't remember leaving them on.

He opened the door and stepped into his house. Everything seemed in order, so he relaxed. He took a shower and settled down by the VCR to watch some kiddie porn. Finally, when he was finished sexually pleasuring himself, he realized how tired he was. It was past midnight. All he had to do was go to the bathroom and then head straight for bed.

He relieved himself, then flushed the toilet. A bomb exploded at that very instant and Clark was thrown clear across the bathroom as the walls came tumbling down right on top of him.

When the police arrived, there was nothing left of Mr. Long for them to save.

CHAPTER SIX

A pile of discarded tissues lay beside Vicki's bed and she struggled to open another box. Damn this summer cold! Her head felt like it was about to explode and she could barely breathe. But the time in bed gave her an opportunity to think about one of her patients: Lawrence Taylor. She had been treating him for several weeks now and it was stirring up all kinds of feelings inside her. Passionate feelings. Sexual feelings. She would sit there trying to listen to him but mentally wondering what it would be like to be kissing him, holding him. The more she tried to deny these feelings, the stronger they became. There was only one thing she could do.

Stop seeing him. Sure, that would bring up his feelings of abandonment, but it was the best thing to do. He would be better served if he were to consult with another psychiatrist.

Someone knocked on her door. Dragging herself out of bed Vicki went to answer it. It was her friend Sue.

"Hi Vic," Sue greeted her. "You look terrible. Still sick, I see."

"I feel terrible."

"I brought you over some chicken soup. Home made. Get back into bed. I'll go heat some up and bring it to you."

"Thanks," she crawled back under the covers. Soon Sue served her a steaming cup of broth.

"You'll never guess who I ran into the other day," Sue said.

"Who?" Vicki took a sip of the hot liquid.

"Dave."

"How's he doing?"

"He says he's doing great. But you know what? I bet if you were to give him a call, he'd come running back to you."

"Thanks, but no thanks."

"C'mon, Vicki. Give him a call. It's not like you have men lining up and beating your door down. There's no other man in your life, is there?"

"No," Vicki answered.

"You hesitated. Are you not telling me something?"

"I'm not seeing anyone."

"But there is someone you're interested in, isn't there?"

"Oh, Sue. I suppose I can't hide it from you."

"What is it?"

"I've got a crush on one of my patients!"

"No," Sue gasped.

"I've tried to deny it, believe me. I feel I'm somehow a bad psychiatrist, a weak person, for letting a patient affect me this way."

"You're neither of those things. You're only human. It's crazy though. Of all the men you've dated, you never had any feelings towards them. Now you have feelings, but it's for the wrong man."

"What am I going to do? I can't continue to treat him."

"No, you shouldn't."

"I'll give him a month to see another psychiatrist. That should be enough time for him to find someone else," Vicki decided.

Larry sat in a movie theater trying to concentrate on what was playing. Some ex-policeman was trying to prevent the hi-jacking of a jetliner. Yet he couldn't get into it. Something was interfering with his concentration. Something he had tried to put off dealing with for the last several weeks.

He was in love with his psychiatrist. That day when she had spilled the can of Pepsi on him, he felt an attraction towards her. He had wanted to ask her out right then, but felt too shy. Now seeing her once a week furthered those feelings. He felt so confused, but there was only one thing he could do. On his next appointment, he was going to have to tell her how he felt.

On the day she finally was over her cold, Vicki went back to work. She got through the morning and had only two patients left to see this afternoon. Carrie Graden and Lawrence Taylor.

Carrie had just been released from MassMental and Vicki was not sure what to expect. She was pleasantly surprised.

"Something changed in me since I left MassMental," Carrie explained. "After you visited me that day, I was ashamed of how I had acted. I decided I really do want to get better."

"I'm glad to hear that."

"So I'll be cooperating with the treatment from now on."

"What made you decide?"

"I can't go on living my life as I had been anymore."

"Tell me about your life."

"There's something wrong with me, I've known that for years now. I used to lock myself in my room for no reason and cry. I still do. For some reason, I can't get it together."

"What was your childhood like?"

"It was terrible. At school, I always felt different. Other kids would make fun of me. They called Chub-ette, because of my weight. They had other names for me too. Names too painful to reveal."

"That must have hurt you deeply."

"It did. Especially since there were fatter kids in the class nobody picked on."

"So they singled you out."

"It would seem so. That's one of the reasons I dropped out of high school. Boy, did my parents freak! You'd have thought I committed mass murder or something."

"Even your own parents couldn't understand what you were going through."

"They knew I was hurting, but they couldn't understand it. This is going way back, but once when I was only six, my folks had company and were sitting in the living room. I took a steak knife from the sink, walked over to my mother, and asked her to stick it in my stomach and kill me."

"What did your mother say?"

"She tried to laugh it off, like it was funny or something."

"She didn't take you seriously. How did that make you feel."

"Worse. I always felt nobody understood me, now I knew even my own mother didn't."

"So even since you were in first grade you felt different?"

"Painfully so. I hated myself, hated my life and hated the world."

"You must have felt like the world hated you too."

Carrie thought about it. "Exactly."

"Your parents didn't understand you, your classmates made fun of you. Have you ever had anyone in your life who cared about you?"

"I had a boyfriend once, but he fell in love with someone else and left me."

"So even someone you cared about, had a relationship with, caused you pain."

"I feel like I'm cursed or something. I'm never going to be happy," Carrie sighed.

"It's important that we examine your life so you can learn from your past. It will probably be very painful confronting many aspects of your life. You may even feel worse as our time progresses because so many things will be stirred up. But I believe you're a strong woman, Carrie, and that you can feel better about yourself and go on to lead a mostly whole, happy life."

"So you're not mad at me at the way I threw that pillow at you at MassMental?"

"Of course not," Vicki laughed. She talked with Carrie a while longer and set another appointment for her, pleased at the way Carrie had opened up to her today. Perhaps there was hope for Carrie.

Her next client was Lawrence Taylor. She broke out in a sweat. It was going to be difficult to tell him she could no longer treat him. "How are you?" she asked him as they seated themselves.

"Getting better, I think. I haven't had any more nightmares this last week."

"Terrific."

"It is. It's all because of you."

"Actually, you did all the hard work."

"No, it's because of you. I know you're helping me a lot. In fact, I think about you often."

"What are your thoughts?"

"That I like you. That I like you a lot. I've liked you ever since that day you spilled the can of Pepsi on me. I should

63

have asked you out that day. Sometimes I wonder, if I were to discontinue therapy, would you go out with me?"

"I think what you are going through is transference. All patients go through it to some degree or another," she explained, her heart beating a mile a minute because Taylor also had feelings for her.

"I feel like such an idiot sharing these feelings with you. After all, what if you don't feel anything towards me? What if you secretly hate me or something?"

"This is the place to bring up such feelings," Vicki choked. "However, today I have something I need to discuss with you. I've reserved four more sessions for you. After that, I won't be able to treat you any longer. We need to spend some time discussing what this separation will mean to you. I've printed out a list for you with the names of other psychiatrists in this area you can consult. You may want to begin calling them this week."

Larry sat there in shock. He was dumbfounded, barely hearing her words. Absently, he took the list Vicki handed him and scanned through it. "But I don't want to stop seeing you. Don't I have any say in the matter?"

"I'm afraid you don't. I'm cutting back on my hours," she lied, "and I just don't have the time to see you anymore."

"But . . . but . . ." Larry stammered, staring out of the bay window.

"What are you thinking?"

"As if you care," Larry spat. "For weeks now I've sat here, spilling out my problems to you. Now you want to pass me off to some other doctor like I'm some used book."

"That's not true. I just think your needs would be better served by seeing another psychiatrist at this time."

"Screw it. Screw it all!" Larry stood up. He tore up the list Vicki had given him into countless little pieces. Then, he flung them at her. Like snowflakes in a winter scene, the papers floated downward, landing on the floor and on Vicki's hair and clothing.

"I think we need to talk about this," Vicki said sternly as she shook off the pieces of paper.

"I think not. There's nothing to talk about. I've fallen in love with you and you don't share my feelings. End of story. Don't bother saving the next four appointments for me. I won't be there."

"I'll keep them open in case you change your mind," Vicki said as Larry turned around and stormed out of her office. The phone suddenly rang, startling her. "What!" she answered it in a loud voice, not in the mood to speak with anyone.

"Vic, are you O.K? It's me, Sue."

"Oh, hi Sue," Vicki flopped down on the sofa in her waiting room.

"What's wrong? You sound awful."

"It's that patient I've told you I've fallen for. He was just here."

"You told him you couldn't see him anymore?"

"I explained it to him. I told him I was cutting back on my hours and suggested he start looking for another shrink."

"How'd he take it?"

"Sue, he's in love with me too."

"He's what?"

"He's attracted to me too. I think we both knew that day we collided in town. He told me he wanted to discontinue our therapy so he could ask me out."

"Wow. Of course you can't see him though. That would be totally unethical."

"I know. Don't remind me. Anyway, I think this is it. He told me he's not going to come in for any of the last four appointments I've set up for him."

"We shall see," Sue hesitated.

Kimberly Long thought about Tony's offer all night and all of the next day. What choice did she really have but to take Tony up on his offer? Sure, she could stay in hooking and wind up like Shawna. She loved Shawna, but she did not want to still be a hooker at age thirty. What Tony was offering her was a new chance at life, a life taken from her by Clark Long.

She had to give Tony an answer. Picking up the phone, Kim took a deep breath and gave Tony her decision. Yes, she would let him take care of her and would give attending Boston Central University a chance. It wasn't as if she had too much too lose. She didn't want to continue living with Sandy if Angel was around. A college dorm room sounded just fine to her about now.

Vicki had almost forgotten about Larry when his fourth and last set-aside therapy hour arrived. In that respect, she almost hoped Larry wouldn't show up. It would only rekindle her desire for him.

A sickening crunch of metal against metal jolted her from her thoughts. She rushed to the bay window of her office and looked down. A taxicab had collided with an MBTA bus on the street below, but no one appeared seriously hurt. Vicki saw several policemen rush to the scene and take charge. While one began to redirect traffic, the other four occupied themselves taking statements from the parties involved. A crowd of people was gathering to watch.

There in the crowd! There was Larry Taylor, making his way to her office building. She felt like she may faint. Apparently Mr. Taylor did plan on keeping his final appointment with her. She tried to calm herself. In several seconds he would be here. The termination of their therapeutic relationship had to be handled as professionally as possible.

She gave him a minute to settle down in the waiting room before she opened her office door. "Mr. Taylor. Won't you come in, please."

"I wasn't going to come," Larry took a seat opposite her. "But I had to."

"I see. Have you made arrangements to be seen by somebody else?"

"No. I've been doing a lot of thinking though. I'm really sorry for the way I acted last time we met. But I am serious. I would like to get to know you better. This is our last session together. I realize you probably think it's unethical, but I think you have feelings for me too. Don't ask me how I know. I can sense it, that's all."

"The concern I have for you is the concern I have for all my patients."

"I don't believe you."

"Mr. Taylor, I won't discuss this any longer. I've already done what I can for you. I've given you the names of several fine doctors in this area, a list you most inappropriately tore up. I'd be glad to replace the list for you if you promise not to repeat your previous behavior."

"That won't be necessary. Shrinks are a dime a dozen in the phone book," Larry muttered, leaving her office.

Suddenly Vicki heard him scream and she ran out to her waiting room. Larry was sitting on the floor, rubbing his ankle.

"My ankle! I think I've sprained it," he said with a look of pain. "Can you help me over to the coach so we can take a look at it.

"Sure," Vicki responded, helping Larry rise to his feet. Unsteadily, with her help, they made it over to the sofa.

In one swift motion Larry held her tight and kissed her.

The kiss was everything as she had so often imagined it would be. It totally engulfed her, beckoning for her to surrender to her desires. Only through the utmost self-control and willpower did she manage to pull back. Her body was trembling. "I can't do this," she somehow uttered. "We need to talk about what just happened." The words came out rushed and nervous. For the first time, she understood what patients meant when they said they felt unreal. This was exactly how she felt.

"You lied to me when you said you had no feelings for me," Larry whispered. "The way you kissed me back, I can tell that you do."

"No! What just occurred was inappropriate. It should never have happened," she tried to pull back from his grasp, but he held her close. "You're the one who's lied. You never had a sprained ankle, did you?"

"No," he kissed her once more.

This time as their lips met, Vicki did not attempt to pull away. All her mental reasoning and ethics flew out the window as she melted into his arms, clinging to him as she would a life preserver in a stormy sea. Gently he undressed her and she in turn undressed him. They made wild, passionate love on her waiting room sofa, each thrust of his sending her into never before experienced heights of ecstasy. They made love for hours and hours, losing all sense of time.

Finally, Larry spoke up. "Do you regret sleeping with me?"

"As your shrink, this should never have happened," Vicki said, lying on top of him and still wrapped in his arms.

"You're my ex-shrink. I'm not your patient anymore," he reminded her while caressing her body.

"It doesn't matter," Vicki answered half-heatedly, as her desire began to build for him again. "I had a certain responsibility to you and I blew it."

"I'm the one who took advantage of you," Larry told her. "Anyway, does it matter? We're both attracted to each other. I want to get to know you. I want to be with you. We do have a lot to discuss, including what just happened today. Let's say we start getting to know each other better over dinner tomorrow night."

"You got it," Vicki agreed. She had crossed an invisible boundary line by having sex with a patient. There was no turning back now.

CHAPTER SEVEN

"I can't believe it!" Vicki's best friend Susan shouted loudly. "You actually slept with him?"

"It wasn't anything I had planned on doing," Vicki lamely tried to defend herself.

"Right. I suppose he took advantage of you."

"In a way he did. He pretended to sprain his ankle in my waiting room. As I was helping him, he kissed me. The next thing I knew, we were making love on the waiting room sofa."

"This is nuttier than any soap opera I've seen. Have you considered how this could all damage him? After all, this man is your patient."

"Was my patient. Lawrence Taylor is no longer my client."

"Vicki, that still doesn't make it right. What if he turns around and sues you? What then?"

"I don't think he will. Anyway, he isn't technically my patient anymore. Sue, I feel as caught up in all this as you are. I never expected any of it to happen."

"So what now?"

"I'm supposed to meet him for dinner tonight at The Olive Garden. In fact, I better hang up now and go get ready."

"Vicki, I really hope you know what you are doing."

When she arrived at The Olive Garden, Larry was already seated at a booth and sipping a drink. "Don't worry. It's only diet coke," he told Vicki as she took a seat.

"I wasn't worried," Vicki exclaimed. She felt nervous meeting him out of the office for the first time, and noticed he seemed nervous also.

"Nervous?"

"You read my mind," Vicki took a sip of her water.

"I am too," Larry admitted.

"I guess I'm overwhelmed by what occurred between us."

"So am I."

"I'm the one who's at fault. You were my patient. I should never have allowed what happened to occur in the first place."

"Please. I'm not your patient anymore. Can't we start over? I'm very interested in you. I'd like to begin dating you. Would you like to get to know me better?"

"I feel I know you already through our sessions together."

"You know a part of me. There is so much more to me. I had a mid-life crisis that you helped me get over. I'm feeling better than ever now. You once told me I needed to focus on enjoying the many years I have left in this life. I want to spend that time getting to know you better, doing things together. You wouldn't have come if you considered our liaison yesterday a one night stand."

"I'm so confused," Vicki rubbed her temples. "I'm torn between doing what is right and what feels right in this case. I suppose after yesterday I can't pretend any longer. I would like to get to know Lawrence, the whole man. I do want to spend time with you and I'm very much attracted to you. But we have to go slow and analyze every step we take. I don't want to do anything to inadvertently harm you."

"We'll take it one day at a time," Larry promised.

"Look—the leaves are already changing color," Vicki exclaimed two months later as she and Larry strolled on a walk through the Boston Common.

"Well, it is autumn," Larry pointed out. Suddenly Vicki stopped and bent down. She fished a peanut out of her pocketbook and held it out directly in front of her. Fascinated, Larry watched as a squirrel timidly approached and grabbed the nut out of Vicki's hand. Leave it to Vic to remember to bring peanuts for the squirrels, he mused as more squirrels circled around her.

"Aren't they cute?" she looked up at him and smiled.

"Adorable," he smiled.

When she ran out of nuts, the squirrels all ran away. Vicki stood up and brushed any remaining peanut shells from her slacks. Arm in arm the couple continued on their walk through the Common. "I think autumn is my favorite season," Vicki declared.

"Even better than summer?" Larry was surprised.

"Every season is my favorite as long as I get to spend it with you," she replied. "I'm so glad you'll be moving in with me this month. Then we can spend all our mornings and nights together."

"I want to be with you. I've fallen in love with you."

"The feeling is mutual," Vicki smiled. All her hesitations and second thoughts about the relationship had vanished.

"Mutual enough to marry me?" Larry asked.

"What!" Vicki shrieked.

"I'm serious. I'm asking you to marry me. Victoria Moore, do you love me, Lawrence Taylor, enough to take my last name and marry me?"

"Stop joking," Vicki nudged him as they walked.

"I'm not joking," Larry insisted.

"Then, you Mr. Taylor, have got yourself a wife."

Kimberly Long had two words for college life: it sucked. Definitely, positively, absolutely, she did not fit in. Even after many weeks of trying, she had yet to make one friend. However, true to his word, Tony was paying for everything and she was out of the Zone. She figured she should at least try to make a go of it. Yet she missed Sandy and Shawna. At least they understood her. Here at Boston Central University she had no one.

Her next class was Economics. After weeks of sitting in on the class, she still didn't have but the vaguest of ideas what it was all about. Fortunately, she was doing better in her other classes.

A little bit late, Kim arrived at the Economics classroom and slid into an empty seat. The professor scowled at her before resuming his lecture. She tried to avoid his gaze.

Her mind drifted, and she found herself deciding on which major to study. Kim closed her eyes, picturing herself as an attorney. Nope. That's not what she wanted to be. A teacher? No, she couldn't picture it. A physical therapist? Maybe, but that didn't feel exactly right either. A nurse? What about training to become a registered nurse? She visualized herself working in a big, metropolitan hospital, actually turning her life around and helping people. She liked the idea. Liked it a lot, as a matter of fact. If she were to stick this college thing out, she'd like to become a nurse.

Her daydreaming was not lost on the instructor. "Ms. Long. Kindly explain how we calculate the GNP?"

She opened her eyes. The entire class was staring at her. "I'm . . . I'm not sure."

"Could it be because you had your eyes closed and were in La-La land the entire time I've been lecturing?"

"I'm sorry," Kim stammered, searching for an explanation. "I was feeling rather tired."

"Tired? You're tired, I'm tired, the whole classroom's tired. What a pitiful explanation. I'm warning you people, all this stuff's going to be on your final exam, so I expect you to know it. I certainly hope the rest of you are paying more attention than our very own Ms. Long."

Kim felt totally humiliated. She hated the way Mr. Allen had singled her out in front of the whole class. When the hour was up, she was the first one out the door. She wanted to get as far away from Boston Central as possible. So she was rather surprised when she felt someone tap her shoulder from behind.

"Don't let Mr. Allen get to you," a pretty brown-haired girl told her. "That's just the way he is."

"Oh," was all Kim managed to say.

"I should know," the girl continued. "This is my second time taking his class. He failed me the first time around."

"He's such a jerk. Most the time I have no idea what it is he's talking about," Kim added.

"You and half the class. My name's Denise Carpenter, by the way."

"Kim Long."

"I was wondering if you'd like to get together and study sometime?" Denise asked.

"That would be great," Kim answered enthusiastically. Her first friend!

"Here, take my number," Denise gave her a slip of paper. "I live off campus, not too far away from here."

"Thanks," Kim said, handing Denise the number of her dorm room phone.

"I'll give you a call," Denise promised.

"Great. I'm free all the time," Kim added, hoping Denise really would call her.

The remainder of the semester passed quickly for Kim. She and Denise became great friends. They would spend their evenings studying or roaming the campus looking for things to do. It was a good time for Kim, reinforcing her decision to finish college and become a nurse. She even passed Mr. Allen's class. That was like icing on the cake. Granted, all she got was a lousy 'C', but at least she'd be putting that horrid class behind her.

The Holiday season was getting into full swing, so Kim and Denise decided to go shopping downtown one day. They took the trolley from Boston Central into town and got off at Park Street. From there, it was only a block to all the major stores. Filene's and Macy's both had spectacular window displays. Christmas carols were being sung on the corner of Winter Street by some church group. Adding to the atmosphere was an ice sculpture of Santa and all his reindeer. "Imagine all the work it took in creating this ice sculpture," Denise mused.

"Yeah. But it was worth it. It's beautiful," Kim agreed. "Let's go hit some stores. I'm getting cold."

"O.K. But I want to take another look at the sculpture before we leave," Denise said.

For the next several hours both girls amused themselves shopping at most the downtown stores. "What do you want to do now?" Denise asked after they looked the Santa ice display over again.

"We can go to the Enchanted Village at City Hall Plaza before going home," Kim suggested.

"A great idea, my buddy and pal," Denise led the way.

There was a long line snaking to the Enchanted Village tent when they got there. Kids were running around all over the place and clamoring to get in.

"What do you say?" Kim asked. "Do you want to wait in line? We can always come back some other time."

Denise was about to reply when suddenly a hoarse voice boomed behind Kim. "Well, if it isn't Slim Kim? How you doing, Kimmie?" There was only one person who called her Slim Kim or Kimmie. Alfred, her old cheapskate trick from Boston's Combat Zone. Sure enough, when Kim turned around, he was standing right behind her.

"Aren't you going to introduce me to your friend?" Alfred grinned.

"Let's get out of here," Kim tried to lead Denise away, but Alfred grabbed her coat.

"What's the matter, Kimmie? Old Alfred not good enough for you anymore?"

"This man knows you?" Denise was confused.

"OH, I know Kimmie here real well, real well indeed," Alfred smirked. "She's my girl," he squeezed Kim harder. "Where are you two ladies heading? I can drive you there and make it worth your while. I got a hundred bucks. What'll that buy me?"

"What is he talking about?" Denise asked Kim.

"Nothing," Kim tried to twist free of Alfred's grasp. She would literally die if Denise knew of her past life as a prostitute. She didn't know if Denise would understand.

"C'mon, Slim Kim. What's a little blow job for an old friend and customer?"

"You're a prostitute?" Denise asked Kim.

Alfred let Kim go. "Hey—I didn't know your friend was a rookie. I'll catch you some other time, Kim," he limped away.

"Is it true? Was that disgusting man really a customer of yours?"

"Denise, I can explain . . ." Kim began.

"You really don't have to," Denise began to walk towards the Government Center trolley stop. "What you do with your personal life is really none of my business."

"But that's just it," Kim caught up to her friend. "I'm not hustling anymore. That's in my past. I'm going to school now. I want to make something of my life. We've become such good friends. I don't want anything to change that. Please, won't you let me tell you my story?"

"O.K." Denise stopped. "I thought I knew you but I was wrong. Let's go grab a hot chocolate and you can tell me about your life's been like."

"What do you have in these boxes, rocks? Vicki complained as she lifted one up.

"Books," Larry corrected her. "I'm a big reader and I never can bring myself to throw a book away."

I guess not," Vicki agreed, peeping into the back of the U-Haul truck Larry had rented to transfer the last remaining items from his apartment to her. It was stacked with boxes and boxes of books, everything from old textbooks to the latest novels. "At least you have a wide range of interests, judging from these books."

"We can sort through all this stuff later. Let's just get it up to your apartment."

"Our apartment," Vicki corrected her future husband. They spent the rest of the day moving boxes and rearranging the Brighton apartment.

It was extremely hard for Kim to have opened up to Denise. She told her friend all about her life in the streets and how uncomfortable she felt attending Boston Central. Over the hot chocolate, as Kim bared her soul, Denise had seemed very interested and supportive. Naturally, Kim had insisted Denise tell no one. The last thing Kim wanted was for word of her private life to be gossiped all over campus. Her friend assured her she wouldn't breathe a word to anybody. Having Denise know all this information about her made Kim nervous, but she had come to trust Denise.

Kim sighed as she packed a suitcase in her dormitory. The dorms were virtually empty now. Christmas vacation had begun and most students had already left to spend the holidays with their families.

"Bye, Kim," a red-haired girl peeked into Kim's room.

"Bye, Gina," Kim waved, wishing she had somewhere to go for the holidays. For a minute she considered spending it with Sandy, but then she remembered Angel was living with Sandy at her old apartment. No way. Spending Christmas with Angel would be like spending Christmas with a disease.

Tony's place at the Prudential Towers was out of the question also. For a man with no social life, Tony claimed to be busy on Christmas Day.

Looked like she was spending Christmas Day at Howard Johnson's motel in Kenmore Square, not to far from Boston Central. That's where the university housed the few remaining students who had nowhere to go over vacation. It was cheaper for them rather than keeping all the dormitories open.

She grabbed her suitcase and walked down to the motel along with a school representative and a small group of students who would also be staying there during winter break. Inside the lobby, they were assigned their room numbers.

"Is there a swimming pool, gym, or game room here?" one of the students inquired hopefully.

"No," the representative snapped. "Now, if there are no more questions, we'll see you people back in your dorms after the New Year. Enjoy your stay."

"Yeah, right," the student mumbled as the group dispersed.

The room assigned to Kim was no luxury suite, but at least it was warm and clean. She unpacked her suitcase, putting her clothes neatly inside the drawers and hanging some in the closet. It was weird. This was the first time she had ever been in a hotel room and there wasn't any trick to turn. Her loneliness was so great she wouldn't have minded even if there was. What she needed was for something to take her mind off her predicament. She put on an old sweatshirt and baggy pants, leaving the motel to go jogging along the Charles River.

"You look great," Larry reminded Vicki as she checked herself in the car's rear view mirror for the hundredth time.

"I don't know," Vicki murmured uncertainly. "This lipstick doesn't quite match my dress."

Amused, Larry rolled his eyes. "I'm sure no one will notice."

"I want to look my best before I meet the people you work with," Vicki applied some bronze eye shadow. "Are you sure my hair looks all right?"

"It looks great," Larry playfully ran his fingers through her long blonde curls.

"Stop it or you'll mess it up," Vicki gently slapped his hand.

"Sorry," he apologized. "Can we go in now?"

"Wait," Vicki answered, taking a small vial of perfume out of her handbag. Generously she sprayed each wrist. "Now we can go in," she determined, climbing out of the passenger's seat and closing the car door.

"You're sure now?" Larry teased. "I wouldn't want you to have forgotten anything."

Vicki bit her lip. "No, I think that's everything. Hopefully I'll make a good first impression with your co-workers."

"You always make a good first impression," Larry gave her a kiss. He draped his arm around her as the walked towards the restaurant where Ideal Advertising had booked their annual night-before-Christmas party. Inside, their ears were greeted by cheerful Christmas music.

"Take your coats?" they were asked.

Both of them checked their coats in.

"Remember, whatever you do, don't tell anyone you were once my psychiatrist," Larry whispered.

"Mum's the word," she promised.

"That's Mr. Andrews," Larry pointed to an overweight man piling a plate sky-high at the buffet table. He's such a bore. He's cheating on his wife, Ginger, but I think she knows."

"Lawrence, my boy," Mr. Andrews called to Larry as he and Vicki approached the buffet table. "And who is this pretty thing?"

"Mr. Andrews. I'd like you to meet my fiancee, Victoria Moore."

"Fiancee? I didn't even know you had a girlfriend tucked away somewhere."

"Yes. Vicki and I are engaged."

"Engaged? Did I hear Larry say he's engaged?" a distinguished looking older man approached the trio.

"Yes. Vicki, this is my boss, Mr. Josh Hillman," Larry introduced them.

"Vicki. What a pretty name," Mr. Hillman admired her heart shaped engagement ring. "Congratulations. I'm so happy to hear Lawrence will finally be settling down. Please grab a plate and come join my wife and me at our table."

"We'll be glad to," Larry said. "Whereabouts is your table?"

"It's the center table directly in front of where the band is playing."

"We'll be over in a little while," Larry promised.

"Everything looks so appetizing," Vicki admired the delicacies arrange on the buffet table as they filled their plates.

"The food at these parties is always good."

"Larry!" someone else called his name.

He turned around. "Hi, Harvey. This is my fiancee, Vicki Moore. Vicki, I'd like you to meet Harvey Wilkerson. Harvey does the graphics at Ideal."

"Nice to meet you," Vicki shook Harvey's hand.

"Likewise," Harvey gave her hand a vigorous shake. "I guess this means for sure Larry's partying days are over."

"Don't worry. I promise not to rein him in too much," Vicki laughed.

"Well, I just came up to the buffet to get my girlfriend some more shrimp," Harvey explained. "I'll see you guys later."

"Are you ready to go sit down?" Larry asked Vicki.

"Just let me get another scoop of this lobster salad," Vicki piled some more on her plate. "O.K. I'm ready."

They made their way across the crowded floor over to Mr. Hillman's table. He pulled out a chair for Vicki to sit down first then seated himself.

"Vicki, I'd like for you to meet my wife, Claudia," Mr. Hillman introduced her to a plain looking woman beside him. "Claudia, this is Victoria Moore. She's Larry's fiancee."

"Nice to meet you," Claudia smiled.

"Likewise," Vicki smiled.

"How did you two meet?" Claudia asked Larry.

Larry knew to expect the question. "We met through a mutual friend."

"This engagement seems to have occurred so suddenly," Mr. Hillman observed. "Surely you both haven's been dating for all that long?"

"Long enough for me to decide Vicki's the woman for me," Larry answered.

"Josh and I dated for two years before settling down," Claudia spoke.

"What sort of work do you do?" Hillman asked Vicki.

"I'm a psychiatrist. I have a private practice in Boston."

"A psychiatrist! I would never have pegged you for a shrink. You must hear all sorts of problems in an average day."

"I like to help people."

"Still, anyone who consults a psychiatrist is bound to have a lot of problems," Hillman reasoned.

"That's true, but sometimes people get better."

"If you ask me, young lady," Josh continued, "you would have to be nuts to see a psychiatrist. I don't care what anyone says. I don't believe in it."

"I've seen people lead normal lives thanks to psychiatry," Vicki explained. "There are all sorts of new drugs available for mental illness for the people who need to be on them. Psychiatry isn't just talk anymore."

"I believe people improving is the exception rather than the rule," Hillman continued to disagree.

"Anyway, we're both just so glad Larry has finally found someone he can relate to," Claudia tried to change the subject.

Her husband picked up on the hint. "Excuse me," he said, rising from his chair. "I think I'm going to ask the band if they could play a little dance music. All this good food has really weighed me down."

"That's a wonderful idea," Claudia agreed. "I'd love to dance. What about you, Vicki? Do you dance?"

"Not very well, I'm afraid."

"I'll show you a few steps," Larry offered. "It's real simple."

For the next several hours they danced the night away. "Hey, this is fun," Vicki admitted.

"I love you," Larry whispered into her ear as he pulled her close.

"I love you too," she whispered back.

"May I?" Hillman tapped on Larry's shoulder to cut in. "You're a wonderful dancer," he told Vicki as they twirled around the dance floor.

"Larry was just showing me a few steps."

"Then you're a fast learner. I forget. How is it that you and Lawrence met?"

"We met at a party through a mutual friend," Vicki lied.

"I think you and Larry will be very happy together. As I'm sure you know, he's a great guy. A few months ago I think he had some kind of personal crisis where he wasn't getting any sleep and was rather depressed, but he's a lot better now."

"You don't say," Vicki smiled.

"Switch?" Harvey Wilkerson waltzed alongside of them with his girlfriend. Soon Vicki was in his arms.

"Having a good time?" Harvey inquired.

"A great time. Everything's perfect. All this dancing is getting me tired though. I think I'll sit down after this one."

"So when's the wedding?"

"Soon. What about yourself? Any plans for tying the knot?"

"Naw. I'm too committed to the playboy lifestyle. Maybe someday. I'm not like Mr. Hillman. He thinks everyone should get married."

"He probably has a very happy marriage."

"Yeah, but not everyone does. I like Josh. However, he has a firm sense of right and wrong he's always trying to get others to conform to."

"In other words, he's too overprotective."

"Something like that," Harvey mumbled, whirling Vicki around the dance floor. In a few seconds, the music stopped playing and the band announced a break.

"Finally," Vicki said with relief. "I've had it. That's it for me. Thanks for the dance. I'm sure this won't be the last time we see each other." Harvey bid her farewell and went to join his girlfriend at the buffet.

"You look tired," Larry noticed as Vicki returned to the table.

"Exhausted," Vicki told him.

"Would you care for some coffee?" Claudia pointed to a fresh pot placed on the table.

"Why not?" Vicki poured herself a hot cup. For the rest of the night, she alternated between the dance floor and the table. Only when the party was breaking up and countless good-byes later did she and Larry pick up their coats and leave.

"I'm so tired," Vicki complained once they were in the car. She took off her shoes and rubbed her feet.

"So am I."

"Your boss, Mr. Hillman. I lost track of how many times he asked me to dance."

"I should have warned you. He loves to dance and when he finds a willing partner he sinks his teeth in and won't let go."

"Now you tell me!"

When they got back to the apartment, Vicki went straight to bed.

"Don't go to bed yet," Larry sat down at the edge of the bed and tickled her feet.

"Stop that," Vicki warned him.

Larry pranced upon her, pinning her underneath him. "I have a Christmas gift I want to give you."

"Now?" Vicki yawned.

"It's past midnight so now it's officially Christmas Day."

"O.K." Vicki sat up in bed. "Bring it on. I'm never to tired to open gifts bearing my name."

Larry left the room and returned with a small, gift-wrapped box. Vicki shook it every which way, but could not figure out what was inside it.

"Give up?" Larry asked eagerly.

In answer, she ripped the paper off and reached inside, pulling out a bank savings book. Puzzled, she opened it. Thirty thousand dollars were deposited in the account.

"It's for us," Larry explained. "It's money I've been saving for something important. I want us to use it as a down payment on a house. What do you say, future Mrs. Taylor? Are you up to some house hunting?"

"I'm ecstatic," Vicki fell into his arms. "This is great. I've never had a better Christmas gift."

"Quick. Spur of the moment. Where in Massachusetts would you like to live?"

"Well," Vicki drawled, getting into it. "I've always loved Newton."

"Newton it is," Larry declared. "Newton is a wonderful, thriving community. I'm sure we'll find the perfect house for us there."

CHAPTER EIGHT

Christmas Day. Kim sat in her room at the Howard Johnson's watching it snow outside. The fact that it was snowing somehow made her feel even lonelier. Here she was, on Christmas Day, with nowhere to go. She tried to call Tony, but as before, there was no answer. She was jealous. Jealous he had somewhere to go and she didn't. "This sucks!" she cried in exasperation. She couldn't wait until school started again and she could move back into the dorm. At least there the loneliness didn't sting quite so hard.

Out of desperation, she turned on the television. That's how she'd spend Christmas Day. In bed watching Christmas cartoons. With such entertainment, it didn't take long for her to doze off. Blissfully she was unaware of everything until the ringing of the telephone woke her up.

"Ms. Long?" a professional sounding woman's voice inquired.

"Who wants to know?" Kim yawned.

"Is this or is this not Ms. Kimberly Long?"

"It is."

"This is Ellen Stavis at the Howard Johnson's front desk. There's a police officer here to see you. I told him he could wait in the ballroom until you come down."

There was no reason Kim could think of why a cop should be asking to see her. "Did he say what he wanted?"

"No he did not. You'll have to come down and ask him yourself."

"Where is the ballroom?"

"On the second floor and to your right. I wouldn't keep the man waiting too long."

"Thanks," Kim hung up the phone. It didn't make any sense at all. Why would a cop be asking for her? She hadn't turned any tricks in a long time, so she figured that couldn't be it. With considerable apprehension, she took the elevator to the second floor.

The entire floor was deserted. The only sounds came from her muffled footsteps on the heavy green carpeting. The ballroom was at the end of a narrow, dark corridor. Her shadow cast eerie, distorted images on the walls as she walked towards it. Suddenly she had an unsettling thought. What if there was no Ellen Stavis or any police officer? What if the sole purpose of the call was to get her out of her room? Someone could be robbing her hotel room this very minute!

Kim paused by the brass doors leading into the ballroom. There seemed to be noises coming from inside. She was here. She might as well check it out. Taking a deep breath, she opened one of the brass doors and stepped inside. Darkness greeted her. Why weren't the lights on?

"SURPRISE!" a loud chorus of voices sang out as someone turned the lights on. What was going on? A huge red banner hanging across the room spelled it out for her.

MERRY CHRISTMAS KIM, it read. It was a surprise party for her. And she could spot the person responsible standing in the center of the room. It was Tony. Denise stood by his side surrounded by plenty of other college students.

Before she had a chance to walk over to Tony, Denise ran up to Kim, giving her a hug. "How about it, Kim? Were you really surprised?"

"Are you kidding? I nearly jumped out of my skin. Aren't you supposed to be spending Christmas with your parents though?"

"I spent the morning with them, then I came here. Tony and I have been planning this party for weeks. He's the one who came up with the idea and I invited all my friends."

Tony came over to Kim. "I hope you like our little surprise."

"You guys are great," Kim told Tony and Denise. "My two best friends in the world."

"The two of you thought of everything," Kim looked around the room. A band was playing Christmas music and a bunch of kids were crowding the buffet table. The rest were either sitting down at the tables or mingling among themselves. A brightly decorated Christmas tree stood in the center of the room, right underneath where the banner hung. Nothing seemed to be missing except . . .

"Ho! Ho! Ho!" Santa Claus came bellowing into the room.

"I can't believe it," Kim rolled her eyes. "You guys even went out and hired a Santa Claus."

"Of course. It wouldn't be much of a Christmas without Santa Claus, now would it?" Tony chuckled.

"C'mon. I'll introduce you to some of my friends," Denise took Kim by the hand and led her to a group of people gathered around the Christmas tree.

"Kim, this is Jane," Denise introduced her to a petite, attractive girl. "Jane's studying to become a marine biologist."

"Nice to meet you," Jane smiled.

"And this is Rita. She's in her third year at Boston Central. Rita's studying to become a R.N."

"Really?" Kim perked up. "That's what I was thinking of doing."

"You remember Paul, right Kim? He was in our economics class."

"I'm the kid who always sat in the back," Paul said.

"I remember. How'd you make out in the class?"

"I got a 'C'," Paul frowned. "What about yourself?"

"The same," Kim told him. "That Mr. Allen was such a jerk, wasn't he? I hated that class."

"Hey—it can't be any worse than the economics class I just got through taking back home," an extremely attractive kid joined in the conversation.

"Kim, I'd like you to meet Kyle," Denise introduced them.

"Hi," Kim smiled shyly.

"Kyle is staying with Paul over the winter break," Denise told Kim. "He goes to the University of Chicago but has been thinking of transferring to Boston Central."

"I like it here in Boston," Kyle admitted, smiling at Kim.

"You could live with me," Paul said. "I have a spare bedroom."

"First I have to see if they accept me. I've already seen Northern University, but I haven't been given a grand tour of Boston Central yet. Is that where you go, Kim?"

"Yes."

"Would it be possible for you to show me around."

"Most of the campus will be closed due to winter break," Kim explained. Was Kyle asking her out on a date? She'd never been on a real date before.

"That's all right. I only want to get a general idea of how the school's laid out. We can go for dinner later. What do you say?"

"I think my friend is asking you out on a date," Paul said. "You notice he didn't ask me to show him around."

"I guess I could show you around," Kim agreed. It would be fun to go out on a real date and she liked Kyle.

"Great," Kyle smiled happily. "Where do you want to meet? I haven't rented a car here so any place you can take the train to will be fine."

"How about meeting in the motel lobby here tomorrow at two. We can walk down."

"Super," Kyle smiled.

Denise steered Kim away from the gathering and introduced her to other people. Finally they got some eggnog and sat down together at a table. "So what do you think of Kyle?" Denise asked.

"He seems like a nice guy. Very good-looking."

"I met him one other time when he was in Boston," Denise revealed. "Actually, I'm a little jealous of you. I was hoping he'd ask me to show him around. I've developed quite a crush on him."

"Then I'll cancel tomorrow's date," Kim suggested. "Maybe then you could have dinner with him and show him around."

"Don't do that," Denise insisted. "Obviously he must like you if he asked you out. I'm a mature adult. I can handle it."

"Are you sure? I mean, it's no problem for me cancel."

"Don't be silly," Denise clenched her teeth. "All you're going to be doing is showing him the university, right? It's not really even like a date. So it's no big deal. However, at Paul's earlier we were all discussing plans for New Year's Eve. Everyone had plans but Kyle and me. I was hoping to spend First Night with him."

"Of course he'll ask you," Kim said confidently. "I'm a complete dud. In fact, I've never been on a real date before.

Once Kyle finds out how boring I am, he'll come galloping to you."

"I hope so," Denise sighed.

"I promise, after tomorrow you'll have him all to yourself," Kim laughed. "Ours is going to be the dullest date in history."

"All I care about is New Year's Eve. I really want to spend it with Kyle."

"I doubt the subject of New Year's Eve will come up at all. Even if he does ask me, I'll tell him I have other plans."

Denise thought about it. "No. If he asks you out, you should go with him. I don't want to play second fiddle."

"You're placing me in an awkward position," Kim complained. "I don't feel comfortable doing anything with Kyle now, knowing how you feel."

"Let's just forget it," Denise said lightly. "He hasn't asked either of us to celebrate New Year's Eve with him yet. Besides, there are plenty of fish in the sea. Sooner or later I'll find someone who I'm interested in who's also interested in me."

"Don't write Kyle off just yet," Kim reminded Denise.

"Let's play it by ear. Forget I said anything," Denise said quickly as another girl joined them at the table. "Kim, this is Carol. Carol helped Tony and me coordinate this party."

"If only you could have seen the look on your face when the lights came on," Carol told Kim. "You looked like you had seen a ghost or something."

"I was totally surprised by this party. I thought I was being set up or something."

"You were. Only it was us setting you up for this surprise Christmas party."

"You're the girl who called me pretending to be Ellen Stavis, the Howard Johnson's operator," Kim figured out by means of Carol's professional-sounding nasal voice.

"You got it. I knew I could pull it off because I work part-time as an operator at Boston Central."

"Certainly, you have the voice for it. Do you go to school at Boston Central also?" Kim asked.

"No. I go to M.I.T., but they didn't have any operator positions available. I study robotics there."

"That must be interesting."

"It's fascinating. It's absolutely amazing what robots can be programmed to do. Why, I bet in the future robots can be manufactured that are smarter than human beings."

"I think there are robots now that are smarter than certain human beings," Kim stated seriously.

"I know what you mean," Carol agreed. "It's absolutely amazing how stupid human beings can act some of the time."

"Some of the time? Try most of the time," Denise rejoined the conversation, as they all started to laugh.

"What's so funny?" a tall girl standing nearby wanted to know.

"Nothing," Denise sobered up. "Kim, I'd like you to meet Pamela, but everyone calls her Pam."

"Hi, Pam."

"So what's everyone laughing at?" Pam persisted.

"Nothing," Denise repeated. "It's not even that funny. We were just talking about how stupid people can be at times."

"Speaking of stupid, did you know Jerry locked his keys in his car? He's out there in the snow trying to get it open," Pam said.

"Need I say more?" Denise shrugged.

"Have you made any plans for New Year's Eve yet?" Pam asked Denise.

"Not yet," Denise answered glumly.

"Too bad. If Kyle asks you out, you can double with Tom and me for First Night."

"We'll see."

"I finally got that damn car door opened," a heavy kid approached the table. He was covered with snow.

Pam laughed. "Kim, I'd like you to meet Jerry. Jerry, this is Kim. Jerry's an expert when it comes to providing us all with comic relief."

"Nice to meet you," Kim smiled.

Jerry brushed some snow off his jacket. "I'm going to get some hot chocolate. Care to join me, Pam?"

"Sure," Pam followed him.

"Now that's what you call an odd couple," Carol commented. "Pam is so smart, and Jerry, well, he's Jerry. I seriously doubt he could think his way out of a paper bag."

"He can't be that bad," Kim wondered.

"Oh, no? You'll see when you get to know him better. The kid is six donuts short of a dozen."

"So what does Pam see in him?"

"Beats me," Carol answered Kim. "Maybe she feels super smart when she's around him or something."

"Listen guys," Denise yawned. "I hate to break up the party, but I promised my folks I'd be home early. Carol, do you think you could introduce Kim to the others she hasn't met yet?"

"No problem."

"Great," Denise gave Kim a hug. "Merry Christmas. I want you to go out and have a great time with Kyle tomorrow. Otherwise, I guess I won't see you until school starts. We have a lot of classes we're in together this coming semester."

"Good. I'm going to need someone to study with."

"See you after the new year then," Denise added.

"Definitely. Thanks for going through the trouble of helping Tony set up this party. I really appreciate it and I had a great time."

"That's what friends are for," Denise said.

When Denise left, Carol introduced Kim to the other college students. Kim had a great time even though she knew she'd never remember everyone's names. It was late when the party started to break up and the rest of the crowd went home.

"Did you have a good time?" Tony asked Kim now that they were alone.

"I had a wonderful time. I met so many people, thanks to you and Denise."

"I know how hard it's been for you. If there's anything else I could do, let me know."

"You've already done so much for me. Thanks to you, I have a new chance in life. I've even decided what I want to study."

"Which is?"

"Nursing. I want to become a registered nurse."

"That's fabulous. You'll be the best nurse ever. There's so many people you'll be in a position to help."

"That's why I want to do it. I guess deep down I've always wanted to help people in some way."

"I couldn't be happier for you than if you were my own daughter. You've made me a much happier man. I was miserable until you came into my life."

"I guess we need each other," Kim said practically.

"You are so right," Tony agreed. "I'd do anything in the world for you."

When Kim finally made it to her hotel room to retire for the night she felt happier than she had in a long time. She had Tony in her life, new friends, and a purpose: that of becoming a nurse. She quickly showered and changed into a pair of pajamas. Stifling a yawn, she plopped into bed and turned out the lights. She was half-asleep when for the second time that day, the phone rang. "Hello," she sleepily muttered.

"Hi, Kim. I hope I'm not bothering you."

"Kyle?" Her heart beat faster.

"Yes. Denise said you were staying at the motel. Are we still on for tomorrow?"

"I've been thinking, wouldn't you rather have someone else show you around Boston Central? Denise, perhaps?"

"Denise is a nice girl, but I'd rather have you show me around. I think you happen to be an even nicer person."

Kim was flattered. "Is that so?" she played with the cord of the telephone.

"It's very much so. So tell me, how is it you're spending Christmas night cooped up in some motel room? Don't you have family or anything?"

"Both my parents are dead," Kim said, remembering that her father died in some freak explosion recently.

"I'm sorry to hear that."

"Everyone has to leave the dorms over winter break when Boston Central shuts down. If you're one of the unlucky ones without a place to go, they book you into HoJo's. It's cheaper for the school. They don't have to keep the dorms open for only a handful of students."

"I see."

"Actually, I could have stayed with my uncle," Kim explained. She hated lying to Kyle, but under no circumstances whatsoever did she want Kyle to learn of her past. "However, he told me he had other plans. I never guessed until today that those plans were throwing a surprise Christmas party for me."

"I'm glad he did. Otherwise I may never have met you."

There was no mistaking it. Kyle was interested in her and the feeling was mutual.

"I'm glad we met too."

"Well, I guess I won't keep you any longer and let you get back to sleep. See you tomorrow at two?"

"In the HoJo's lobby. I'll be waiting," Kim promised.

The following afternoon at two, Kim entered the motel lobby to wait for Kyle. Feeling nervous, she took a seat in one of the worn out chairs facing the window. Nervously she tied and untied her shoelaces. When she looked up again, there was Kyle, rushing towards the motel.

"I hope you weren't waiting too long," he panted, "but I got on the wrong trolley and had to do a little backtracking. How are you doing?"

"Fine," Kim answered.

"It's real windy outside," Kyle told her. "What's that saying you guys have? If you don't like the weather in New England, wait five minutes and it'll change."

"That's what they say," Kim laughed, happy to be with Kyle.

They left the motel lobby and walked along Commonwealth Avenue. "This is the School of Nursing," Kim stated when the first building on campus came into view. "That's where I'll be going."

"You'd make a dynamite nurse," Kyle said supportively.

"What are you majoring in?"

"Accounting. My father was an accountant and his father before him was. You could say it runs in my family because my mom is also an accountant."

"At least you have people to ask if you have any questions."

"I haven't failed an accounting exam yet. It's nice having both parents knowledgeable in the same field I'm studying."

"That's the Communications building coming into view," Kim pointed. "Directly behind it is the School of Engineering."

"Is the library around here too?"

"The main library is further up the street. It's a drag we can't go inside any buildings because they're closed."

"That's fine. I'm enjoying myself walking around like this. I'll be back to Boston again soon."

"So you are thinking of studying here?"

"Hopefully, yes. What are some of the good sections to live?"

"Beacon Hill and the Back Bay are real nice areas to live if you can afford it. Then there's Brighton. It's called College-town by the locals because of all the students living there. Allston is pretty reasonable rent-wise also."

"What is that building on the right?" Kyle asked.

"It houses four schools. The School of Management, the School of Liberal Arts, the School of Theology and The School of Art."

"What's the Athletic Department like?"

"Not too bad. I hardly get a chance to use it though. Boston Central likes to pile the homework on thick and that's what I spend most of my free time doing."

"I hear you. Where I go, they pile it on thick too."

"That's the Student Performance Center," Kim pointed out a round orange building. "Next to it is the Student Union. There's a food court inside the Student Union, but like everything else around here, it's closed."

"Are you hungry?" Kyle asked.

"A little."

"Is there anyplace close to grab a bite to eat?"

"Not really, Why don't I show you the other buildings and then we'll go for dinner."

"O.K."

For the next hour they wandered around the campus with Kim pointing out any places of interest. Just as she was showing him The Department of Music, a strong gust of wind made off with her headband, blowing it clear across the empty expanse of the campus. Her long, black hair blew haphazardly in all directions.

Kyle took off after Kim's headband, spotting it beside a tree. But before he could reach for it, a powerful wind scooped it up and sent it flying across Storrow Drive. Once more Kyle went after it, this time victoriously clutching it and returning it to Kim, who was fighting a losing battle to keep her hair out of her eyes.

"Thank you," she said gratefully, using the headband to push her hair back. "I absolutely hate my hair on windy days like these. It's so thick and goes all over the place."

"I think you have beautiful hair," Kyle assured her, gently touching it. He leaned closer and Kim instinctively closed her eyes as he kissed her. It was a powerful kiss and the intensity of it surprised her. It felt so good.

Slowly, Kyle pulled back. "What are you doing New Year's Eve?"

"I'm not doing anything."

"I'd like to take you to dinner and maybe we can do First Night and watch the fireworks later."

"I can't do it."

"Why not? You just said that you didn't have any plans."

"I don't. Truthfully, it's because of Denise. Wouldn't you rather spend New Year's Eve with her?"

"No. As I told you, Denise is a nice girl. But she's not someone I want to get to know better."

"That's because you hardly know her. Denise is sensitive, intelligent, funny . . ."

"I'm sure she's all of those things," Kyle interrupted, "but that doesn't change the fact that I don't want to go out with her."

"She's been a great friend. I want her to be happy."

"How about us? Don't we deserve to be happy too? I appreciate your loyalty to a friend, but I'm sure I'm not the first guy to ever reject Denise. It's part of life. We all get rejected sometimes. It's happened to me and I'm sure it's happened to you. Please. I want to spend New Year's with you. Say you'll go to dinner and First Night with me."

Kim felt torn. "I wouldn't feel right."

"Would it be right for me to spend the evening with Denise when my heart wouldn't be in it?"

"No. I guess not," Kim thought about it.

"I want to go with you. You want to go with me. Let's at least make each other happy and spend it together. Your friend Denise will get over it, I'm certain of it."

"She did finally say she doesn't want to play second fiddle. That if you ask me, I should go with you."

"There you go. You shouldn't feel bad making your own choices. I plan on renting a car and I'll pick you up on New Year's Eve at seven. If it's O.K. with you, I'd like us to have dinner at the Pier on the Waterfront. Afterwards at midnight, we can watch the fireworks go off at Boston Harbor. How's that sound?"

"Great," Kim agreed, deciding to go with Kyle. A part of her did not feel comfortable with the decision, but Kyle was right. Denise would get over it. She really hoped so.

CHAPTER NINE

The day before New Year's Eve, Tony phoned Kim to see if she wanted to go to a party on that day. It would be at the luxury hotel he used to own, The Majestic. Kim found it hard to say no to Tony, but she told him she had already made other plans. Tony was happy for her; glad she was making new friends. He told her that as much as he didn't want to go without her, he might pop into The Majestic around midnight anyway.

When Kyle picked Kim up on New Year's Eve, Kim thought she detected the smell of alcohol on his breath. "Have you been drinking?" she asked.

"A little. It is New Year's Eve, after all." He admired her red silk dress. "You look nice."

"You do too," Kim admired Kyle's blue suit. "Blue's definitely your color."

"It's cold outside. You better put a warm coat on."

She pulled out a white wool coat from the closet. "How's this?"

"Perfect," Kyle smiled. "By the way, I saw Denise today," he informed her as they walked to his rental car.

"You did? So she knows that we're spending New Year's Eve together."

"I told her."

"What did she say?"

"She said we should try and have a good time."

"Really? What were her plans for tonight?"

"I don't know. She didn't say."

"Was she mad that you weren't spending it with her?"

"She didn't give the impression she was mad or anything."

When they arrived at the Pier on the Waterfront, the parking lot was full, but soon a space opened up near the entrance. "Shit," Kyle swore, realizing it was a handicapped space.

Kim was somewhat surprised by Kyle's expletive. It seemed out of character for him. "Relax," she said lightly. "We have all night."

"I know. But our reservations are for eight," he informed her. Just then a couple emerged from the restaurant and walked towards their car. They pulled out and in an instant Kyle pulled into the vacated spot. "Are you hungry?" he asked.

"I think I was born hungry," Kim laughed.

Once inside the restaurant, Kyle ordered a bottle of champagne for them to split. At first Kim protested, saying she was underage, but then decided to have some after all. The champagne left her feeling giddy. It had been a long time since she sampled anything alcoholic. When she was working the streets, she never drank. But Kyle wasn't a trick, she reminded herself, and she did not need to stay in control.

Kyle ordered another bottle in the middle of the meal and continued to keep her glass filled. It was almost like he was trying to get her drunk. Finally, Kim had enough and refused anymore refills.

"Did you enjoy your meal?" Kyle asked.

"Very much," Kim giggled as a result of the champagne. "The lobster pie was great. I wish," she told him, "that this night didn't have to end."

"We still have the fireworks to go to."

"That's on Boston Harbor, right."

"Yep. Right across from the Aquarium. Maybe we should leave now. That First Night is pretty popular," Kyle reasoned.

Several minutes later, they were seated in a warm car traveling on the crowded expressway. Suddenly, Kyle turned right and got off at the next exit. "Where are you going? Kim became concerned. "That sign said South Boston."

"It's a shortcut," Kyle explained.

They were traveling along Day Boulevard. In front of them were no cars. Kim turned around and looked out the back window. No cars were behind them either. "This will take us to Castle Island," Kim realized. "You can't see the fireworks too clearly from there."

"We've still got time to make First Night. I thought it'd be nice if we parked and looked out over the water for awhile." He drove the rental car into the parking lot of Castle Island and parked beside the water. "It's nice down here, don't you think?"

"Yes," Kim replied, feeling uneasy. She looked around. Still no other cars were in sight. "Look, let's just go to the Aquarium. The sooner we get there, the better view of the fireworks we'll have."

"What's your hurry?" Kyle put his arm around her. "I thought you liked me."

"I do. But we've both been drinking. Let's leave before we do something we might regret later."

"Regret?" Kyle laughed. "Listen to you. Do you regret sleeping with all the tricks you've gotten it on with too?"

"What are you talking about?" Kim turned to confront Kyle. She tried to wiggle out from underneath his arm. She was not having a good time anymore.

"You don't have to pretend anymore," Kyle looked her straight in the eyes. "Denise told me everything. She told me how the two of you ran into that disgusting john of yours downtown, that you're nothing but a prostitute, servicing hordes of horny men. Well, I've got news for you. I'm horny." With his left hand, Kyle attempted to pull down his zipper, but it was jammed.

"Denise lied to you. She told you that because she's jealous you're not with her," Kim tried to distract Kyle.

"Sorry. Denise sounded convincing to me," he grabbed Kim's hand and placed it on his crotch. "Just think. We can have our own fireworks right here," Kyle breathed heavily.

"Stop it!" Kim tried to pull her hand free and fight off his other hand that was reaching for her breasts. "I want you to take me back to the HoJo's right now!"

"No way," Kyle tried to overpower her. "I'm hungry for you, Kim. I know you want me. What's the big deal? It's nothing you haven't done before."

Kim looked around. Still no other cars in sight. That meant she was alone with Kyle in a deserted parking lot in a part of the city she didn't know very well.

In an instant Kyle managed to un-stick his zipper and he placed Kim's hand on his erect penis.

"Stop it!" Kim scratched at his face with her long nails.

"You little bitch!" Kyle hissed as he hit her.

Realizing if she stuck around, Kyle could really explode in violence, Kim unlocked the car door and jumped out. The cold, salty air of the ocean assaulted her nostrils and sent her hair whipping around in all directions.

SLAM! Kim heard a car door slam. Kyle had just gotten out of the car.

"I'm sorry," Kyle pleaded. "I got carried away. If you get back in the car, I promise I'll drive you back to the motel you're staying at."

"Don't come near me," Kim warned. After what happened, she did not trust Kyle anymore.

"I said I was sorry," Kyle repeated. "C'mon, Kim. Get in the car."

"No," Kim stated firmly.

"What are you going to do? Freeze out here by yourself? There's nobody else around."

"I'll take my chances."

"Get in the car Kim," Kyle ordered, moving closer to where Kim was standing.

In an instant Kim took off, running along a paved path parallel to the beach. She could hear Kyle's heavy footsteps thumping behind her. There was no way she could dream of out-running him. Taking a chance, Kim turned right and ran into the residential section of South Boston. Maybe she could lose him or get help there.

Kyle continued to run after her. Out of breath and tired, Kim forced herself to run even faster. Not a single light was on in any of the triple-decker houses she had run past. However, somewhere in the distance, she could hear the sound of heavy rock music being played. Kim altered her path, running in the direction of the music.

"Will you stop?" Kyle shouted as he chased her. "I'm not going to hurt you."

Fat chance. There was no way she was going to let Kyle catch her, not after the way he assaulted her in the car.

"Give it up, Kim," Kyle shouted. "You're not going to be able to out-run me."

Kim realized he was right. She was becoming more and more tired as she struggled to stay one step ahead of him. Her only hope was to reach the house the rock music was coming from.

Exhausted, she made it to the house and raced up the splintering wooden stairs, stumbling towards the doorbell. With a shaking hand, she pressed it as hard as she could. Nothing. Only then did she see the sign. DOORBELL BROKEN. PLEASE KNOCK. Desperately, Kim started banging at the door with her fists. Behind her she could hear the old stairs creak. Kyle was coming up the stairs to get her. Kim fruitlessly pounded on the door even louder, wondering if anyone inside would be able to hear her above the loudly playing music.

A strong, masculine hand landed on her shoulder and she nearly jumped out of her skin in fright. Mentally, she prepared herself to do battle with Kyle.

"You got to go in through the back," a strange voice boomed in back of her.

Slowly Kim turned around and looked into an unfamiliar man's face. "Huh?"

"You got to go in through the back," the stranger repeated. "You're here for the party, aren't you?"

"Yes," Kim lied, weak with relief. Three houses down she could see Kyle sitting on someone's steps. He was glaring at her.

"Here, give me a hand with some beer," the man asked her once they were on the sidewalk. He walked over to a nearby van and handed Kim two six-packs and grabbed a couple for himself. They proceeded to walk through the yard to the back entrance of the house.

"Are you a friend of Mark's?" the guy asked. "I've never seen you around here before."

"I'm a friend of a friend."

Inside the house was crowded the smell of marijuana hanging heavily in the air. A lot of people were paired up and in various stages of making out.

"Just put the beer on the kitchen table," the man instructed Kim.

She did as she was told. "Is there a phone in here I could use?"

"On the wall behind you," the man watched her.

Trembling, Kim punched in the number of one of the local cab companies.

"Where do you need a cab sent to?" a gruff dispatcher demanded.

Good question. She had no idea where she was.

"Excuse me," Kim asked the man whose beer she helped carry in. "Can you tell me the number and street of where I am?" The man continued to suspiciously look at her.

"Please," Kim begged. "I don't have time to explain. All I'm trying to do is get home."

He must have sensed her desperation. "267 P Street."

"Thank you," Kim repeated the address to the dispatcher.

"Hey! Who are you?" the man demanded.

"I was just leaving," Kim explained. "Thanks for letting me use the phone." Without further explanation, she went outside to wait for the cab. She dared not leave the yard until the taxi pulled up though. Kyle might still be waiting for her.

The waiting seemed to take forever and she shivered from the cold night air. From up above she heard a sudden loud rumble and the sky lit up. The fireworks were going off at Boston Harbor. Spectacular colors of blue, purple and orange seemed to fall to the earth. Kim couldn't witness too much from where she was, but what she managed to see was extraordinary. Each new display seemed to build-on and out-do the one before it and the show continued for roughly twenty minutes. Then darkness. The show was over and once again the stars became the main attraction.

CLICK! Despite the music it sounded like someone on the sidewalk had just kicked a can. She stood very still in the dark backyard, scarcely daring to move. Illuminated by the overhead streetlight a man entered her field of vision. It was Kyle. She heard him cough and than saw him slowly reach into his back pocket and withdraw a pack of cigarettes. He stuck one in his mouth, lit it, and walked away. Cautiously Kim tiptoed to the front of the yard to see where he had gone. Unbelievable. Kyle was sitting on the rickety wooden steps of the house, barely ten feet from her. She dared not move.

Suddenly a car turned down the street. Good. It had to be the cab. But it wasn't. Kim was startled to see a patrol car stop where Kyle was sitting, but not nearly as startled as Kyle appeared to be.

"Hey—kid!" an officer rolled down the window and shouted. "We've gotten a couple of complaints of the loud music coming from this address. When you finish your smoke and go back inside, make sure you tell them to either keep the stereo off or the volume low. Got it? I hate coming back to the same address twice."

"Yes, sir," Kyle gulped. "I'll tell them."

"You better," the officer responded.

Kim smiled. This was her chance to get away. She leaped from the secure darkness of the yard and was about to run to the patrol car when another vehicle pulled up to the address.

It was the taxi she had called earlier! Briefly she decided what to do. She could file a complaint against Kyle, but he'd be out the next day and it would be her word against his. Making a decision, Kim ran and climbed into the cab.

"Where to, Miss?" the driver asked.

She didn't want to go to HoJo's. "The Prudential Towers," she told the man. In the distance she could see the figure of a frustrated Kyle get smaller and smaller. Only when he was out of view did she begin to relax. She had succeeded in out-smarting him.

A half-hour later the cab pulled up to the North Tower. She paid the fare and rushed into the lobby. A sleepy security guard sat dozing behind the sign-in desk.

Kim asked him to ring the penthouse suite for her.

"Sorry, Mr. Whiting's not in," the guard stated.

"I'll wait," Kim said. It wasn't long before Tony stepped into the lobby.

"Tony!" Kim ran up to him. "I've never been so glad to see you."

The surprise of seeing her there caught Tony off guard. "Kim, what are you doing here?"

"It's a long story," tears ran down her cheeks.

"There, there," Tony brushed them away. "Why don't we go up to my apartment and you can tell me all about it?"

"O.K." Kim nodded her head.

She told Tony everything that had happened. How Denise had betrayed her trust. How Kyle had tried to force her into having sex with him and of her escape. Tony listened intently. Just as he had his partners of The Group take care of Clark Long, he'd see to it Denise and Kyle paid for their actions.

"I never want to step foot in Boston Central again," Kim told Tony. "I'm not going back."

"Are you going to give up on your education? Please don't do that. Don't let Kyle and Denise take that from you."

"No. I'd never give them the satisfaction of bringing me down. I still have my heart set on becoming a nurse. I want to transfer to Northern University and start fresh. No one there knows me. Believe me, I'm not about to go opening my mouth and revealing my past again, no matter who asks. Ever."

"Northern has a good reputation. Perhaps a fresh start would be the best thing for you. I'll see to it you are immediately transferred there."

"I have another request."

"Anything."

"I want to move in here with you. No more dorms."

"Are you sure?"

"Positive. None of the other students understand me. Only you do. Will you let me move in here with you?"

"If you really want to move in with me, I'd love to have you."

"You won't regret it," Kim told him. "I'm really a neat person. I'm great at cleaning, cooking, watering the plants. You name it. I even do windows," she emphasized her final point.

"How can I refuse a deal like that?" Tony laughed. It would be wonderful to have Kim live with him. "You can have what used to be Ami's room. It's the only other bedroom."

"Perfect."

"I know you're upset by what happened tonight, but I want you to know what goes around comes around. Kyle and Denise will live to regret how they treated you."

"You think so?"

"Yes. Someday soon, at that. In the meantime, why don't you go get some rest? In the morning we'll call Denise and find out when Kyle is going back to Chicago."

"O.K." Kim agreed.

The next morning she woke up feeling better, even though her legs were still sore from all that running the previous night. She loved Ami's room. The room was pleasant and cheerful. The walls were painted a lively color of pastel blue and the bed she had slept on was the most comfortable she had ever been on. Most importantly, something about the room felt right to her. She felt like she belonged here, that this was the home she had searched for and finally found. It made her so happy that Tony had agreed to let her live here. She infinitely appreciated his generosity. She threw on a robe she found in Ami's closet and went into the kitchen.

Tony was setting up for breakfast. "Good morning. Are you feeling any better?"

"Much better. You shouldn't have troubled yourself making breakfast. I would have done it."

"No problem," he ran to the stove to flip an omelet. "When I was running The Majestic, I had the privilege of picking up many pointers from some of the top chefs in the country. It's made me a pretty good cook."

"I'll say," Kim said as she took a bite of her omelet.

"Glad you like it," Tony took a bow. "After you eat, I want you to call Denise to find out if this Kyle guy is still around. I don't want him anywhere near you. Then I have to take you to the Towers security office to have an identification card made for you along with a key. That way you'll be able to come and go from here at any time without the security giving you a hard time."

"Thanks again, Tony."

"The reason I wanted you to live in a dorm last semester had nothing to do with me not wanting you to stay here. I thought it good at the time for you to be around people your own age. However I respect and understand why you do not want to live in one anymore. I want you to stay here with me. You're my ray of sunshine, kid."

"I love you, Tony," she told him for the first time.

For him, it was like the world stood still. To hear Kim say that made him the happiest man alive. "We'd better call Denise before she leaves for the day."

"Can you call her? I want nothing to do with her."

"Sure," Tony made the call.

"Hello."

"Hello, Denise. This is Mr. Whiting."

Denise sounded nervous. "What can I do for you?"

"Has Kyle left Boston yet?"

"He's going back to Chicago tomorrow."

"Is that definite?"

"Yes. I've even seen his plane ticket. Why?"

"I don't want that man in the same city as Kim. Thanks to your big mouth, he nearly raped Kim yesterday."

"What? I can't believe it."

"Believe it. If you had never told him that Kim used to be a prostitute, he might never had gotten up the nerve to assault her."

"It just happened. I never meant to blurt out Kim's past to him. The only reason I told him about it was so he would stop liking her. I had no idea he would get aggressive with her."

"The point is you made a promise. You promised Kim you would never tell anyone about the things she told you in confidence and you broke that promise. You should have known your actions could have consequences."

"I was in love with Kyle. I wasn't thinking. Is Kim all right?"

"She's been hurt badly by all of this."

"I'm sorry," Denise stated. "Tell Kim how sorry I am."

"Sorry doesn't cut it in this case," Tony hung up the phone. "Kyle goes back to Chicago tomorrow," he told Kim. "I don't want you going out until after that."

"I'll stay right here in the apartment with you," Kim promised. "I would hate to run into the guy again.

"Don't worry. Soon you'll never have to," Tony smiled.

CHAPTER TEN

Monday. First day of classes at the University of Chicago. What a drag! A weary and yawning Kyle tumbled out of bed. He hated the first day of classes because they bored him. Usually everyone just went around the room and introduced him or herself. Sometimes a professor would hand out a syllabus. Real exciting stuff. Nevertheless, he took a shower and got dressed to face the day. He wished he were back in Boston. Next semester for sure. He had received information from Boston Central and Northern Universities, and in the end decided to transfer to Northern. Denise would be glad to see him back in Boston. Of course, it was too late for Kim.

Kim. What went wrong on New Year's Eve? He was a good-looking, well-built hunk of a man. No doubt a lot better than the scum Kim was probably used to sleeping with. The way she ran away from him. Now that really infuriated Kyle. After all, he was no axe murderer or anything. All he had wanted was a little loving. He was a lover, not a fighter. No use over crying over spilled milk, however. Women were like fishes: there were plenty of them in the sea. Women who'd give up their middle finger to be with him. That was the best part of college.

He looked out of his bedroom window. The weatherman last on the news had predicted a very frigid morning with the rain that had fallen last night turning into ice. He could see plenty of icy spots on the sidewalk below. He'd have to walk carefully on the way to class. He shoved himself into a bulky green parka and left the house.

He didn't make it very far. SPLAT! He slipped on a piece of ice and landed on his butt. Fuck, Kyle cursed. These icy spots were no joke. He'd have to walk a lot more carefully from now on.

It was so freezing cold he wished he had bothered to put on a hat and gloves. Long johns would have been nice too. The wind blowing made it feel like it was thirty below zero. Despite the dangerous icy spots he soon began to walk faster due to the cold. Suddenly the idea of sitting in a nice, warm classroom appealed to him. He was almost there. As soon as the light turned red he could cross the street and arrive on campus. When the light turned red and the sign said 'WALK', Kyle stepped off the curb and began crossing the street. That's when he heard and saw it. A huge truck, out of control, was barreling straight towards him.

Heart pounding, his legs began to react to the signals his mind was sending. With a burst of energy, he began to run. He had to make it to the other side of the street before the truck hit him.

Too bad he wasn't watching where he was going. SPLAT! He slipped on another piece of ice. With a sickening, thunderous thud the truck hit him, sending his body high in the air like some rag doll. With a jolt he landed on the sidewalk a good distance away, his body mangled from the impact. Increasingly he was finding it difficult to breathe. He tried to say something to the people who had begun to gather around him, but nothing came out. Nothing but blood, that is.

Kyle realized he was going to die. Gradually he stopped fighting for each painful breath and surrendered to the peaceful darkness descending upon him. Before the ambulance could get him to Saint Joseph's Hospital, he was pronounced dead. The driver of the truck was never caught.

For Denise, the first day of school was great. She liked the first day of classes because they were pressure-free. No hard assignments, no boring lectures. Most of all, she was glad to be among friends again. All her friends, that is, except Kim.

She didn't blame Kim for transferring out of Boston Central. She would have done the same thing if she were in Kim's shoes. Every day she wished she could take back all the information she had told Kyle about Kim. She couldn't blame Kim for never wanting to see her again.

But Kyle a potential rapist? Denise had a hard time swallowing that. It didn't fit with the picture Denise had of him. Kim must have done something to provoke him. Each time she had seen Kyle he was the perfect gentleman. In fact, she still harbored hope that when he returned to Boston he might be interested in her. With Kim out of the way, perhaps she stood a chance.

Yet it bothered her how casually she had betrayed Kim's confidence. It was the first time she had done anything like that. She regretted it, but it was too late to do anything about it now. Perhaps things had worked out for the best, as now maybe Kyle would be interested in her.

Denise checked her watch. She needed to drop off some papers to the financial aid office before they closed. She walked quickly, wanting to make it on time.

"Hi, stranger," a friendly voice called out.

"Rachel, I didn't see you," Denise stopped.

"Where are you off to in such a hurry?"

"The financial aid office. Can you believe they lost my application for a student loan?" Denise said with disgust.

"They're always doing shit like that," Rachel agreed.

"Well, I got run. Are you doing anything? Why don't I meet you in the food court in about an hour?"

"Sounds good. See you in an hour."

"Bye," Denise waved as she hurried towards the financial aid office. She ran into the building, nearly slipping on the floor a janitor was mopping.

"Be careful," the janitor warned.

"Yeah," Denise mumbled impatiently as she waited for the elevator. It arrived in seconds and Denise got on, pressing the button for the twentieth floor. Slowly the elevator began to go up and Denise relaxed. She would make the financial aid office before they closed for the day.

CLICK! The elevator became stuck just below the twentieth floor. Why me, Denise rolled her eyes. Urgently she pressed the button for the twentieth floor. Suddenly, to make matters worse, the lights inside the elevator went off. Denise panicked. She began to press all the buttons, hoping she' hit one labeled Alarm or Emergency or something. Nothing happened. Sucking in an abundance of air, she released the most penetrating scream she could muster. No help came. What if everyone went home and she remained trapped in this damned elevator all night? Wait a minute. Weren't all elevators equipped with a telephone? Excited by this prospect, she began to feel around the control panel once more. Her hand came across a smooth, round knob near the bottom and eagerly Denise pulled the small door open. Help was just a phone call away!

She reached inside the compartment and gasped. No phone was attached to the dangling, twisted cord inside. The phone! What had happened to the phone? It was almost as if someone had cut it off. Her mind flashed back to the janitor downstairs who had been mopping the floor when she got on the elevator. Could he have cut it? She realized she was being ridiculous. Her nerves were beginning to fray. The elevator jerked to the left. Stay calm, Denise pleaded with herself as sweat began to trickle down from her armpits. This was no time to lose it. Again the elevator trembled. Denise threw herself on her knees and began to pray the Lord's prayer as the elevator swayed wildly. The last thing she remembered thinking before the cable snapped was now she'd never get a chance to date Kyle.

Denise's body was discovered by a maintenance crew the following morning. The malfunction of the elevator remained a mystery.

Within the year, Vicki and Larry were joined as one. The wedding was a simple ceremony attended by their closest friends and relatives. Yet they were still-hunting for their perfect dream house in Newton. One day they received an urgent phone call from their realtor, Martin, informing them he had found the perfect home for the couple. In about half an hour they arranged to meet Martin in front of the Newton residence, which was on the market.

The house was more a mini-mansion. It was elaborate, light blue in color and a lot of land surrounded it. "Pretty nice," Larry whistled.

"So what do you think?" Martin met them as they came out of the car. "Wait until you see the inside. I'm telling you. This is the perfect home. It has everything. It's even got a swimming pool out back."

"How many rooms?" Vicki asked, falling in love with the outside.

"Twelve. Two bathrooms. I'm telling you. The house is perfect." Martin gushed.

The interior was even more impressive than the exterior. The rooms were spacious with plenty of windows for natural light. The tour continued with Martin leading them from room to room. "This would be the perfect room for your psychiatric practice, should you ever want to have it here," Martin stopped in the doorway of a particularly large room. It even had a bay window, just like Vicki's office in downtown Boston.

"What a great idea," Vicki agreed. "I'd love to see patients here."

"So, are you going to buy this place," Martin swooned. "I can make all the arrangements."

"I don't know? Larry—what do you think?" Vicki asked her husband.

"I like it," Larry said. "It feels like home. It's by far better than any home we've looked at so far. Plus, it has this great room for you to move your practice into. Let's take it."

"Sold," Vicki told the realtor. Within a week, they were moved in and enjoying their new home.

Kim Long liked it much better at Northern University than she had at Boston Central. She was glad she made the switch. Even the people seemed much nicer. She thought back on all the people she had known at Boston Central. It gave her the shivers to think of the way Denise Carpenter had died. Trapped in a plunging elevator. How terrible those last few seconds must have been to her. Kim remembered reading there was no phone in the elevator, no way Denise could have called for help. She lay dying all alone in that elevator shaft all night until the next day when maintenance was summoned to fix the broken elevator. As much as Kim despised Denise for her actions over winter break, she never wished for the girl to come to such a horrible end. It was nothing short of a tragedy. She tried not to dwell on it too long, though. For the first time, her life was going great. Straight A's. Those were the grades for every single class she had taken at Northern. She was really proud of herself. Nothing was going to deter her from becoming a nurse.

And nothing did. Three years later, Kim graduated at the top of her class. She immediately found work at County Hospital, a major teaching hospital in Boston, on their Medical East unit. To celebrate her accomplishments, Tony bought her a red Mercedes. Kim loved riding all over town in it and to her new job. She even convinced Tony to take a trip with her to his old summer home in Mount Mooselauke, New Hampshire. Tony vehemently protested, as it brought back memories of Margaret and Ami for him. But in the end, Kim won and he agreed to accompany her. On the way back, they stopped at Denny's for a quick coffee before heading home.

It was while sipping her coffee Kim decided to ask him. "Do you find me attractive?"

"Of course I do. You're a beautiful woman."

"Well, I was wondering. I've been living with you for over three years now and you've never tried to make it with me."

"I've always considered our relationship special as it is."

"So do I," Kim said. "But don't you ever wish for something . . . more?"

"Kim, you look so much like Ami that I wouldn't feel right."

"But I'm not Ami. I'm Kim. I want you to treat and look at me as such."

"I try, honestly I do."

"So what's the problem? Why don't you want me?"

"I don't want to ruin what we have. Believe me, it's not because I don't find you attractive."

"What if I wanted us to be more than just friends?"

"In case you haven't noticed, I'm a lot older than you."

"So what? I've slept with plenty of older men I cared nothing for. I care about you. I've given this a lot of thought. I want to be your girlfriend."

"Someday you're going to find someone you truly care about, then I'll be the one hurt."

"Life is all about risks. I'll never stop caring about you. You've given me my life back. If not for you, I'd still be turning tricks with Sandy and Shawna."

"I'm so glad you're not."

"Then let me show you how glad I am of that," Kim insisted. When the arrived home at the North Tower, she wouldn't let the conversation drop.

"I'm perfectly happy with the relationship as it is," Tony told her for the fifth time. "End of story. I'm going to bed. Don't stay up to late. Remember, you have to work tomorrow."

She lay awake thinking that night about how lonely she felt sleeping in Ami's room all by herself. Restlessly, she got out of bed and wrapped a bathrobe around her slender body. She was going to see Tony. He'd never seen her in the nude. Perhaps that would change his mind.

But Tony wasn't in his room. She found him in the kitchen, eating a bowl of cereal. "I was coming to see you," Kim let the robe slide off her body.

"Sit down," Tony told her. "I'm not prepared to make love with you, but I may as well be truthful. I promised myself I would never reveal what I'm going to tell you. It didn't matter until now, as I was too depressed to have sex anyway. I have this problem, this psychological block ever since my wife died, of making love to any woman. I'm impotent. Completely useless. I can't get it on at all."

"We can try," Kim suggested. "Come with me," she led him into the master bedroom and removed his robe. They both lay down on his bed.

"It's no use," Tony said nervously.

"Relax," Kim instructed, rubbing her body against his. For an hour she tried every trick she knew. Touching. Teasing. Tantalizing. Nothing happened and Tony did not get an erection. But then he felt her mouth upon him, and the blood rushed to the center of his body. Fireworks went off. Millions of them. Tears welled up in his eyes. He felt like jumping for joy. His erection was a miracle, a sensation he thought he'd never get to experience again in his life.

"I thought you said you couldn't get it up," Kim teased, running her hot tongue over his smooth stomach.

"Thank you. Thank you," Tony cried. It was by far one of the happiest days of his life.

CHAPTER ELEVEN

Waiting for her husband Larry to rush home was like waiting on pins and needles. Vicki couldn't help staring at the lottery ticket she had bought yesterday at Sunshine Convenience. After counseling Carrie Graden, she had walked to the convenience store for a sandwich and a quart of milk. Not one to play the lottery, she was about to leave when the clerk informed her the jackpot for the MegaMoney game was one hundred million. So she took a chance and bought ten tickets. Then she forgot about them, until today, when the noon news announced that there were two winning tickets purchased for the big MegaMoney game. The reporter than continued to recite the winning numbers.

Hastily Vicki wrote them down, then checked the tickets she bought to see if any of the numbers matched. Her heart nearly stopped beating! All the numbers on one of her tickets matched exactly. It couldn't be. There had to have been some mistake. Never had she won anything of significance in her entire life. So she called the lottery's pre-recorded winning line and wrote the winning numbers down again. Once more the numbers matched the ones on her ticket. Could it be? Could she have really won half of the one hundred million dollar MegaMoney jackpot? She tried to imagine the scene at Lottery Headquarters when she and Larry arrived to cash the ticket in. There would be reporters, photographers and news people galore. A definite madhouse. Vicki was becoming nervous just thinking about it.

She tried doing some breathing exercises. Slowly now. Breathe in and out, in and out. But it was no use. Who in the world could stay calm in the face of winning fifty million dollars?

Fifty million dollars. Vicki couldn't even imagine how that much money would look like. Would it be enough to fill her kitchen? Her living room? Her entire house? Her entire house including her back yard?

What was taking so long for Larry to arrive anyway? She had called him and told him the good news an hour ago. Shouldn't he have been here by now? She wanted the lottery ticket cashed today.

Nervously, Vicki sat down on the sofa, her crumbled, sweat-stained lottery ticket in her hand. Hard to believe, but soon she'd be cashing in this little piece of paper for a cool fifty million dollars. Her only decision was did she want the payments spread out over twenty years or did she want to receive a lump sum payment instead?

Lawrence Taylor couldn't believe it either. He was still in shock from the phone call he had received from Vicki earlier. Fifty million dollars! Never did he dream his life could get any better than the way it was. Though they were financially well off, he never thought they'd ever be filthy rich. He was floored, totally shocked, when Vicki had called him at his office earlier in the day. She had told him a lottery ticket she purchased yesterday at Sunshine Convenience was one of the two winning tickets to hit the one hundred million

MegaMoney jackpot. Split between the two winners, that meant fifty million Vicki could collect spread over twenty years or as a lump sum payment. His boss, Mr. Josh Hillman was in Larry's office when the phone call came and heard the whole conversation. Larry had mumbled that he was leaving to take Vicki to Lottery Headquarters in Braintree to cash in the ticket and then ran out of his office to his car parked on Winter Street. There he nearly shit. The front right tire was flat. Of all times for something like that to happen. Looking around, Larry noticed a cab in the distance and waved. The driver pulled up and that's where Larry found himself now. In the back seat of a smoke filled cab. If all went well in about one hour he and his lovely wife Vicki would be fifty million dollars richer.

The shower felt splendid. It was nice and hot, just the way Luke Spiros liked it. He used a lot of soap to lather up. A lot of shampoo also, since he never bothered to wash his hair until it was good and greasy. Accordingly, his last shower had been three weeks ago.

He sent the shower nozzle to massage, feeling the very hot water pulsating against his body. It felt good, too good. Lo and behold, he was getting an erection. He'd find someone to take care of it in Boston's Combat Zone later on.

Luke was still enjoying himself in the shower when the phone rang. Cursing at the interruption, he shut the shower off and ran to answer it.

"Yeah," a dripping, wet Luke barked into the phone.

"Mitchell wants you to call him right away," a voice unfamiliar to Luke said ominously.

"I'm kind of naked right now," Luke explained. "I'll call as soon as I shower and get dressed."

"NO! Right now! Call Mitchell right THIS minute. If you know what's good for you," the voice boomed at the other end. Then the line went dead.

Moving at the speed of light, Luke threw on a smelly pair of jeans and an old sweatshirt. He didn't even pause to put on a pair of sneakers. Instead he threw them in a gym bag containing the tricks of his trade to put on later.

Like a bat out of hell Luke tore out of the shabby individual Chelsea Motel cabin he was living at. He didn't have a phone in his particular room because he didn't want to pay for it, but there was a bank of pay phones at the very edge of the parking lot. Frantically digging in his pants for some change Luke headed straight for the telephones. He dropped the needed change into one of them and dialed Mitchell's private number. This must be important. Mitchell answered on the first ring.

"Serpent," Luke muttered a code word, which changed often.

"Here's what I want you to do," Mitchell started to explain.

Vicki had decided. She'd take the fifty million in a lump sum payment. With wise investments it would be a better deal than waiting twenty years to receive what was hers.

Mentally she began to daydream of how she and Larry will spend some of the money. Of course they'd both help their families and give generously to charity. And there was this trip to Australia they often talked about but never made. And wasn't Vicki's car always breaking down? She always did want an expensive car and now she could afford several.

The doorbell rang, causing Vicki to jump a mile out of her skin. What now? She wasn't expecting any company and Larry had the key.

The ringing became more incessant, urgent. Vicki searched for a place to put the lottery ticket while she went to answer the door. She decided to slip it underneath a sofa cushion.

When she peered through the door's peephole she didn't recognize the shabbily dressed young man standing there. "Who is it?" she yelled.

So far so good. For a minute Luke thought her was going to have to break the door down. "I'm an undercover officer," he flashed a badge. "There's been a terrible accident. We must evacuate the area."

Vicki felt her knees go weak. First the shock of winning the lottery and now this? She hesitated. "What sort of accident?"

"There's been a major gas leak. We are in the process of getting everyone out of their homes and into the school auditorium down the street. While you prepare to leave, I have to use your telephone to call my office. Is that O.K., ma'am?"

"I .... guess so," Vicki mumbled. She started to open the door. This was an emergency and the guy had shown her his police badge.

The sound of the door opening was like music to Luke's ears. He fingered the gun in his holster.

"The phone's in the kitchen," Vicki said, stepping away from the door.

In an instant Luke was upon her, painfully twisting her arm behind her back. With his other hand he calmly leveled the gun against her temple. "O.K., Bitch. The winning MegaMoney ticket. Where is it?"

Vicki struggled to breathe. How did this guy know about the winning MegaMoney ticket? She had told absolutely no one but Larry. This was all a dream. Please, please, just let this be a dream.

"Three seconds. You got three seconds to tell me where that ticket is or I blow your brains out. One . . ."

Vicki was terrified. If she told him where the ticket was who's to say he wouldn't kill her anyway?

"Two . . ."

Where was Larry? Why wasn't he home by now? If she ever needed him to walk through the front door it was right this very second.

"Three . . ."

"It's underneath a sofa cushion!" Vicki cried out, tears rolling down her face.

Luke dragged her towards the sofa. "Which cushion?"

"The middle one," Vicki trembled.

Luke lifted the middle sofa cushion. Sure enough, the lottery ticket was tucked underneath.

"O.K. You got it!" Vicki shrieked. "Take it. Just take it and leave."

Luke pushed Vicki away from him and fired, hitting Vicki right in the chest. He fired again. Vicki went down.

Smiling, Luke walked over to where Vicki lay and fired again until he was certain she was dead. That was his favorite part of the job. The killing. Then he ran out of the house.

He drove for miles and miles before pulling next to a pay phone to call Mitchell. "I've got the ticket," he shouted excitely when Mitchell picked up the phone.

"I had faith you'd get it," Mitchell said evenly. "The man and woman. You eliminated them both?"

"Wait a minute," Luke began to panic. "I eliminated the woman. You said to kill whoever was there. There was no man there."

"Christ!" Mitchell said angrily. "He must not have gotten home yet."

"Should I go back and see if I can kill him too?" Luke asked eagerly.

Mitchell hesitated. "Too risky. Perhaps Mr. Taylor won't be that big a problem. If he is, I'll give you the order to take care him too. Just get your ass with the winning lottery ticket over here as soon as possible.

"I'm on my way," Luke promised. "Meantime, don't worry. Just say the word and Taylor's a dead man."

"What seems to the hold up?" Larry wondered. The cab had stopped and all Larry could see up ahead was some kind of traffic jam.

"Don't know," the taxi driver shrugged his shoulders. "Could be an accident up ahead."

Larry sank back in his seat and groaned. Poor Vicki. She must be wondering what was taking him so long to get home. "Isn't there some other way you could go?"

"Not until the Allston/Brighton exit. Once I get there I can take some side streets to your place in Newton."

"Please hurry," Larry begged. He closed his eyes. The smell of heavy cigarette smoke soon assaulted his nostrils. He opened his eyes to see that the driver had just lit up another Camel.

"Can I have one?" Larry asked. Normally he didn't smoke, hadn't for years. However the stress of Vicki winning the lottery and now being trapped in a slow as molasses traffic jam was getting to him.

"Bad habit," the driver passed a crumpled cigarette and matchbook through the partition to Larry.

"Thanks," Larry lit up and inhaled deeply. He passed the matchbook back to the driver through the partition. As he did, the traffic started moving.

"We're in business," the driver called. "What street did you say you lived on?"

"Eliot Green. 32 Eliot Green Street."

A half-hour later the cab made a turn on Eliot Green Street. But something was wrong. The street was swarming with cops. And they all seemed to be clustered at 32 Eliot Green Street.

"That your place?" the taxi driver said. "I don't think I can pull up much closer".

"Thanks," Larry paid the man. He jumped out of the cab and ran towards his address. "What's going on?" he quizzed one of the cops that was standing on his porch.

"One of the neighbors thought she heard some gunshots."

"Gunshots?" Larry pushed passed the cop to go inside.

The cop grabbed Larry by the sleeve. "You can't go in there."

"I live here!" Larry shouted, breaking free and rushing inside. He had to know his wife Vicki was safe.

Blood was all over the living room and seeping through the carpet. In the middle of the floor surrounded by blood lay Vicki. Beautiful Vicki. Dead Vicki.

"Who are you," one of the officers barked.

"Lawrence Taylor," Larry said weakly. His eyes refused to believe what he saw. This was supposed to be one of the best days of his life. It just wasn't possible. He couldn't take his eyes off Vicki lying dead on the floor. And all that blood . . .

"Get him out of here!" the officer ordered.

"Mr. Taylor, come with me," a young policeman put his arm around Larry and gently led him into the kitchen. "We can talk in there."

Obediently Larry followed. He was in shock. Nothing did, nothing could have, prepared him for this.

"Mr. Taylor. Do you know of anyone who'd want to hurt your wife?"

"My wife was murdered for her MegaMoney ticket," Larry mumbled.

"For her MegaMoney ticket?"

"My wife called me at work. She said she had just won the MegaMoney jackpot, that there were two winners and she was one of them." There. He had just given the cops a motive for the murder. He was of no use now. Never in a million years could he get by without Vicki by his side.

"You said your wife called you at work because she won MegaMoney. Did you discuss this with anyone or do you know if your wife did?"

"I don't know about Vicki, but my boss Mr. Josh Hillman from the Ideal Advertising agency where I work was in the room with me when Vicki called me."

"I see."

"Look, officer. I'm not feeling too well. I really need to use the bathroom." He felt ill. Mentally ill.

"Where is it? I'll walk you to it."

"It really won't be necessary."

"No problem," the officer insisted.

The officer told Larry to avert his eyes as the walked past the living room and took the stairs to the second floor. He posted himself outside as Larry went in to use the rest room.

The first thing Larry did was lock the door shut. He had to be quick and quiet. Trying not to make any noise he opened the medicine chest. There was a bottle of some old Valiums inside that he once had prescribed but never took. Shit. It probably wouldn't be enough. Larry poured himself some water in the toothbrush cup and swallowed all the pills. What else could he use? He didn't want to go on living without Vicki. His eyes fell upon an unopened pack of razor blades. Shaking, Larry lifted them from the shelf and held them in his trembling hands. Did he have the courage?

He thought he did. Trying not to make any noise he opened the box up and pulled out a razor blade. The silver edge glistened in the light. He was trembling real badly now. Perhaps it wouldn't hurt as much if he slashed his wrists under cold water?

Larry turned on the cold water. As he was about to slice through his wrist, the blade fell from his hand and plopped into the sink. Gingerly Larry picked it up again.

"You O.K. in there?" the cop yelled. He started banging on the door. "You've been in there a while."

"Be right out," Larry slurred. The Valium was starting to work. It was now or never. First he put his left wrist underneath the water and sliced through it. Then he did the same with the right. Blood flowed into the sink and splattered all over. Losing consciousness, Larry fell to the floor.

Kimberly Long was glad when her shift was over. She loved nursing, but sometimes the long hours and difficult patients got on her nerves. Still, she wouldn't quit nursing for the world. For six weeks now she had worked the inpatient medical unit and was very happy with her job. She loved being a nurse.

"Goodnight," one of the nursed yelled as Kim walked towards the elevators at the end of her shift. Kim waved bye and stopped at the water cooler for a cool drink. Suddenly she heard a man's voice shout her name. Wait a minute. That was Tony shouting her name. What was he doing here?

"Kim, you're not going to believe this!" Tony grabbed her tight and lifted her off her feet.

"What's gotten into you," Kim laughed at Tony's excited state. "You just happy to see me?"

"You're not going to believe this, Kim. You're not going to believe it. I have great news to tell you."

"Believe what?" Kim laughed.

"What would you say if I told you I was one of the MegaMoney winners?"

"You're right. I wouldn't believe you," Kim chuckled. "Come on. Let's go home."

"Kim-I'm serious," Tony looked her in the eye. "Yesterday I bought a ticket at Sunshine Convenience and it hit. You're looking at Boston's newest multi-millionaire. I've come to take you to Lottery Headquarters so we can cash in the ticket."

Kim was speechless. She tried to speak but nothing came out. A million thoughts fluttered through her brain. Her senses all felt scrambled. "This really is unbelievable," she finally spoke with great effort. She felt dizzy and weak. But it was a good dizzy and weak.

"I told you I had great news," Tony smiled. "Madam . . . may I escort you to Lottery Headquarters and then for a celebration fit for a king afterwards?"

"Lead the way," Kim laughed with happiness.

"How are you feeling?" a much too cheerful voice asked.

Larry struggled to open his eyes. The Valium had completely spaced him out. He had no idea where he was or how he got there. In addition, something was binding his wrists. Bandages. "Where am I?" Larry tried to focus.

"You're at the County Hospital emergency room. I'm Dr. Elizabeth Stone. How do you feel?"

"Like I want to die," Larry moaned.

"We had to pump your stomach and bandage your wrists. If it weren't for one of the cops breaking the bathroom door down when you didn't respond, you might not have made it."

"I want to get out of here," Larry decided. To go home and finish the job.

"I'm afraid that won't be possible."

"What do you mean?"

"We'll be keeping you here at County for the night for observation. Tomorrow morning you're being transferred to Harborside."

"Harborside?" Where had he heard of that name before?

"Oh, you'll like it at Harborside," Dr. Stone told him. "It's the best private psychiatric hospital in Boston. They're really good there. It isn't like MassMental or anything; it's a lot better. You'll see."

A psyche hospital! They were going to send him to a psychiatric hospital! "I'm not going!" Larry made that clear.

"I'm afraid you don't understand. You have no choice. The concern is you're still suicidal. There's a court order sending you to Harborside for evaluation for twenty-eight days."

The color drained from Larry's face. "Court order?"

"That's right. It's really for your own good. You'll get all the help you need. I've heard a lot of good things about the place."

"Fuck," Larry swore. The last thing he wanted was to go sit in the nut house for close to a month. Don't worry, Vicki, Larry silently vowed. In twenty-eight days he'd be joining her on the other side. He couldn't wait.

CHAPTER TWELVE

The next day an ambulance deposited Larry in front of Harborside. It was located on many acres of land in a sparsely populated section of Brookline. Why the place was called Harborside Larry wasn't certain, as the large, modern building was no where near Boston Harbor. Perhaps it was at one time before being moved to its present location.

Whatever. He couldn't care less what the history of the place was. He was angry as hell and full of rage at being committed here. No one could understand his pain. The minute they released him he'd only try to kill himself again. Only this time he'd make certain to succeed.

Two hefty, muscular ambulance drivers escorted Larry into the building and to the front desk. The place was impressive inside. Yellow leather chairs took up a good part of the waiting room. Large, colorful paintings hung on the walls, their main color being yellow. Larry guessed the management thought yellow must be a soothing color. Most strange was how quiet it was on the grounds. Larry had figured psyche hospitals to be noisy, hectic places.

A young woman sat behind the front desk. "Hi Paul. Hi Chris," she greeted the ambulance drivers. "Long time no see.

We'll be ready for Mr. Taylor in a minute. Why don't you all have a seat. Someone will be down shortly to take Mr. Taylor to the locked ward."

The locked ward. It sounded so frightening.

Soon an older black man with graying hair strode into the room and walked to where Larry sat. "Mr. Taylor, I presume," he greeted Larry. I'm Melvin Thomas, your main mental health worker during your stay with us. But everyone calls me Mel. If you'll be so kind as to follow me, these two fine men and I well take you up to your unit"

Paul and Chris made small talk with Mel until they reached the second floor unit. Mel took out a key and opened the door. He thanked the ambulance drivers for safely escorting Larry to his destination and locked the door using the key once he and Larry were inside.

"Let me tell you I appreciate why you're here," Mel told Larry. "Who knows how I might have reacted coming home to find out my wife was murdered. The murder's been in all the papers, all the news shows. Such a young woman. So tragic," Mel shook his head.

"Will the police be coming here to interview me?" Larry wondered.

"A detective from the Boston Police Department will be coming by to speak with you tomorrow. I believe his name is Robert Greene. You can tell him anything you think might be helpful. Right now I have to show you around the unit. Your psychiatrist's name is Richard Bellamy. He will be meeting with you in twenty minutes. This here is the day room," Mel took Larry into a sunny room. The view from the windows might have been nice if iron bars weren't blocking it.

The room itself contained many plastic yellow chairs and heavy wooden tables. "This is a multi-purpose room," Mel explained. "This is where all meals get served as well as where all group therapy and activities meet. There's a group therapy meeting after breakfast every day. Of course you'll be expected to attend."

"What if I don't?" Larry rebelled. The last thing he wanted to do was socialize with any mental patients.

"You should attend," Mel recommended. "If you don't they might put down that you're isolating and prolong your stay here. See, the main reason people are here is to prove they're no longer a threat to themselves or society. So play the game, follow the rules and come twenty-eight you're a free man. Of course, come that time you might be so charmed by my magnetic personality that you don't want to leave," Mel smiled, his bright eyes twinkling.

"I doubt that," Larry said. Despite himself, he was beginning to like Mel.

Mel continued the tour. "See that room," Mel pointed to a door with a tiny window built in. "It's called the quiet room. Trust me. You don't want to wind up in there. Do you smoke?"

"Not usually."

"This place will drive you to it. Anyway, should you ever get the urge, behind this door on your left is the smoking room. The door always has to be kept closed so the non-smoking people don't complain. Got it?"

"Got it."

"Good. Any questions?"

"How do I know what time anything is?"

"There's a schedule posted on the back of the door to your room. It'll tell you what time meals, activities and everything is. I'll show you where your room is and then Dr. Bellamy should be ready to meet with you."

Larry followed Mel into a small barely furnished room. He was thankful the color scheme in it was blue rather than yellow. All the room held was a twin bed, a chair and a bureau.

"I should tell you one thing," Mel warned Larry. "Since you have attempted suicide you'll be on a twenty four hour suicide watch. That means either myself or another mental health worker will be watching your every movement like a hawk. That means zero privacy. It'll be up to Dr. Bellamy to determine when you're no longer suicidal."

"Sounds like this Dr. Bellamy is a very powerful man."

"Around here he is. Let's go. He's probably waiting to see you."

Mel led Larry into a one of the meeting rooms near the nurse's station. Dr. Bellamy was waiting inside. He was a relaxed, confident man with dark hair and glasses. In fact, he didn't look much older than Larry's age of forty, even though Larry knew he was probably older than that.

"Dr. Bellamy-I'd like you to meet Lawrence Taylor," Mel introduced them.

"My pleasure," Dr. Bellamy shook Larry's hand. "Please, sit down."

As they seated themselves Mel quietly slipped out of the room.

"I understand you came home yesterday afternoon right after your wife was murdered," Dr. Bellamy stated.

Larry nodded.

"Can you tell me what that was like?"

"It was terrible. I actually saw the body." Larry buried his face in his hands.

"It was then you decided to kill yourself?"

"That's right. I have absolutely no reason or desire to go on living."

"You feel like hurting yourself?"

"Yes."

"Tell me about Vicki," Dr. Bellamy leaned back in his chair. "She was a psychiatrist, am I right?"

"Yes. She had a practice from our home in Newton. Vicki was my whole life. You see, I don't exist without her."

"How long were you married?"

"Three wonderful, happy years."

"Any children?"

"No. We hadn't started our family yet. We were so high on each other."

"How do you envision your life without her?"

"I don't."

"You look sad and depressed."

"That's an understatement," Larry snorted. "Wouldn't you be sad and depressed if your wife were murdered? Doctor, there is something else. This is hard for me to say, but I feel responsible for Vicki's death."

"How so?"

"On the day of the murder Vicki called me at work to come home right away. She claimed she had just discovered she had one of the two winning MegaMoney tickets for the previous night's drawing. I told her I'd be right home so we could take the ticket to Lottery Headquarters to cash it in. I ran to my car but my tire was flat. It took me a long time but I finally managed to flag down a cab. Then we got stuck in a traffic jam. By the time I got home Vicki had been murdered. I feel if only I could have gotten there sooner . . ." Tears rolled down Larry's eyes.

"You feel you could have saved her if not for the delay of the flat tire and then the traffic jam?"

"Yes," Larry admitted.

"That must be a terrible burden."

"I don't want to be alive to bear it. Plus there is one other thing."

"Yes? I know this is hard for you to talk about."

"All this is hard for me. You see when Vicki's call came to my office there was someone in the room with me who heard the whole conversation. My boss, Mr. Josh Hillman heard me discuss the MegaMoney drawing and knew Vicki had hit. I believe he had something to do with the murder."

"You're telling me this Mr. Hillman murdered your wife?"

"No. He probably didn't. But he might have tipped off someone that my wife had won and that person killed her."

"These are serious accusations. You'll definitely get a chance to discuss your concerns tomorrow with Robert Greene. He's the police detective who will be coming to speak with you. I'm sure they'll get to the bottom of this. Meantime, I will be meeting with you every day to assess your situation. Hopefully by the end of your commitment I'll feel comfortable in releasing you."

"I hope so," Larry agreed. Then he could go home and try again to kill himself.

Mel was waiting outside in the corridor when Larry finished his session. "You have a visitor," he stated.

"Mom!" Larry shouted, noticing his distraught mother standing near the nurse's station.

"Larry, oh Larry!" his mother cried as the both ran to greet each other. She wrapped her son in a big, motherly hug.

"I'm so sorry, mom," Larry buried his head against his mother's shoulder. "I flipped. I didn't mean to end up here. But I can't go on without Vicki." For the second time this day Larry wound up crying.

"I understand," Mrs. Taylor soothed her son. "The murder's been in all be papers and news shows this morning.

They said they were bringing you here for observation. I came as quickly as I could. Please Larry. No matter what. Don't ever try to kill yourself again. I've lost a splendid daughter-in-law. I couldn't bear to lose you too."

"I hurt so badly, mom,"

"I know, son. The only comfort I have is knowing that whoever killed Vicki didn't kill you too. I need you. Promise me you'll never, ever attempt suicide again."

"I can't do that."

"You must!" Mrs. Taylor replied firmly, the tears running down her face and mingling with Larry's. "I'm begging you. We'll help each other through this. Don't make me live through burying my only son."

Larry thought about it. He hadn't considered how his suicide would affect his mother. Standing there, holding her, he could feel the pain ripping through her trembling body. She had just lost Vicki. Did he want to add the death of her only son to his mother's suffering?

The answer was no. He couldn't kill himself and put his mother through a living hell. As much as he wanted to end it all he decided he couldn't add to his mother's pain.

"Don't cry, mom," Larry stroked her hair.

"Please. Promise me you won't kill yourself. In twenty-eight days you'll be out of here. I can't live with the possibility of another suicide attempt hanging like a knife over my head."

"I promise," Larry finally said.

Mrs. Taylor's body went limp with relief. "Thank God," she exclaimed. "I'll be coming every day to see you. Is there anything you need? Anything I could bring you?"

"I could use a suitcase full of clothes. They took me here straight from County."

"I'll bring it tomorrow. Anything else?"

"No, not really." There really wasn't much he needed on a locked unit.

"Would you like some magazines or books?"

"Whatever you bring will be fine. Mom, I love you and need you," Larry told her. If he was going to go on living he desperately needed the love and concern of his mother.

"I love you too. If there's anything you need, anything at all, I'll be there for you. We have to help each other through this," Mrs. Taylor made clear before bidding Larry good-bye and leaving the unit.

"Do you mind if I smoke?" Detective Robert Greene asked, standing in the doorway of Larry's small room at Harborside.

"No," Larry answered. "I could use a cigarette myself. But we're only allowed to smoke in the smoking room."

"Lead the way," Detective Greene insisted. There wasn't anybody else in the smoking room so he and Larry took seats and lit up. They would be able to talk freely.

"Did you find whoever murdered Vicki yet?" Larry demanded.

"Nope. But your house wasn't broken into, so it appears your wife must have let in whoever killed her. One of our men mentioned a MegaMoney angle. You said your wife had one of the two winning tickets."

"That's right," Larry affirmed.

"However you did not actually see the ticket. Is that right."

"That's right. Vicki called me at work to tell me she had won. My boss, Mr. Josh Hillman was in the room with me when the call came, so you know I'm not making it up."

"We had a chance to talk with Mr. Hillman. He claims no such call came in."

"He's lying," Larry said angrily. "Can't you see, he's only saying that because he might have had something to do with the murder!"

"So you are the only one who knew your wife allegedly had this ticket."

"Besides Mr. Hillman, that is."

"The two winners have both come forward to cash in their tickets. Bryant Cossetti of Pembroke says he bought his ticket at Pembroke Variety. Tony Whiting bought his at Sunshine Convenience. I don't expect you've heard of either of them."

"Wait a minute. Did you say Tony Whiting bought his at Sunshine Convenience? That's where Vicki told me she had bought hers! The murderer. It's got to be Tony Whiting or someone connected with him."

"Mr. Taylor. What time did you leave work on the day your wife was murdered?"

"I'd say around two-thirty."

"You came right home?"

"Yes, but I was delayed because my tire had a flat so I had to take a taxi. There was a lot of traffic so I must have gotten home around three-thirty."

"You wouldn't happen to remember the license number of the cab you took, would you?"

"No. It was the last thing on my mind."

"Do you recall the company this cab belonged to."

"I think it was a Checker cab, but it might have belonged to Town Taxi. I guess I'm not sure what company."

"How long does it usually take you to get home?"

"Fifteen minutes or so."

"Do you remember what the driver of the cab looked like?"

"Not really. He had an accent and smoked Camels. Like I said, I wasn't paying attention."

"What was your relationship with your wife like?"

"Perfect."

"Was there any fighting or arguments going on?"

"None at all. Why are you asking me all these personal questions? It's almost like you think I somehow rushed home and killed my wife. The person you should be interviewing is Tony Whiting."

"These are just routine questions."

"Should I be getting a lawyer?"

"No need to."

"But you're asking me all these questions like you think I'm involved."

"All we're doing at this point, Mr. Taylor," the detective paused to light another cigarette, "is considering all the possibilities."

CHAPTER THIRTEEN

Kim Long was furious. What the hell was this bullshit? Yesterday had been such a happy day when she and Tony went to Lottery Headquarters to collect his lump sum payment. But this morning a Detective Robert Greene from the Boston Police had been by wondering where Tony got the ticket and if he was acquainted with either a Mr. Josh Hillman or Victoria Taylor. Of course Tony wasn't. The first he'd heard of the Taylor woman was on the news, when they announced her murder. Now this woman's husband was accusing Tony of somehow criminally obtaining his winning ticket. Nonsense! Tony didn't need the money. Was Detective Greene blind? Just look at where Tony and Kim lived. At the prestigious Towers, in a luxury penthouse suite. And no, Tony was not having money problems. He didn't have to, but Tony even showed Greene his bank book and investment portfolio to prove his point. This guy Taylor was insane to make such wild accusations. No wonder he was in the nut house! Didn't that alone tell the police anything? Insane or not, Kim was positively livid at Taylor for smearing Tony name. Angry enough to pay Taylor a visit at Harborside.

"Wake up, sleeping beauty," Mel sat on the corner of Larry Taylor's bed and playfully nudged him.

Larry groaned.

"Come on, now, you don't want to miss breakfast or group therapy. Yesterday Detective Greene was interviewing you. Today you don't have an excuse."

"Leave me alone," Larry rolled over. He wished he could just sleep his four weeks in the nut house away.

"Let's get moving," Mel said more seriously. "Dr. Bellamy is leading today's group and I'm sure he'll be expecting you to attend. Remember what I said about playing the game."

"Fuck," Larry reluctantly got out of bed.

"Now that's more like it," Mel praised him.

"Do you really have to sit here and watch me get dressed," Larry complained.

"Them are the rules. Suicide watch. Don't like it, convince Dr. Bellamy to change your status."

"Right," Larry quickly threw on some clothes.

Breakfast consisted of watery scrambled eggs and mushy, bland oatmeal. After everyone finished eating Dr. Bellamy strode into the room.

"Good morning," he cheerfully addressed everyone. "I'll be leading today's group."

A few people wished him a good morning but for the most part everyone remained silent.

"Why don't we make a big circle with our chairs and introduce ourselves. We have a new patient on the unit."

Larry could feel the stares of all eyes upon him.

"I'm Mick," a teenage kid wearing a Boston Red Sox baseball cap on backwards declared.

"Sheila," a girl beside Mick said shyly.

"I'm Wayne," another teenage kid spoke up.

"Everyone calls me Moe," said another kid,

"Hi. I'm Dolores Kent," a normal looking middle aged woman introduced herself. Larry wondered what she was doing on the ward.

"Stuart," the man sitting near Dolores yawned. "Excuse me. I'm tired."

"I'm Jenifer and I'm being held prisoner on this unit," another woman said.

Larry knew just how Jenifer felt.

"Well, that's our little group," Dr. Bellamy stated. His eyes focused on Larry. "Mr. Taylor, would you care to introduce yourself?"

Not really. "Hi. My name is Larry."

"Would you like to share with the group what brings you here?"

Would you like to jump in the lake, powerful Dr. Bellamy? "I'm here because the day before yesterday I tried to kill myself. My wife had been murdered and I felt I had no reason to live."

"I'm sure almost everyone here can relate to how overwhelmed Mr. Taylor must have felt. Sheila here tried to kill herself when her husband of thirty years died of prostrate cancer. I admit, the circumstances are different, but the sense of loss is the same. Sheila, do you have any suggestions that might help Mr. Taylor cope with the loss and adjust?"

"You just have to take it one day at a time," Sheila said sadly. "It isn't easy. I'm still very depressed and on medication. Perhaps something like Prozac would help Larry."

"No," Larry shook his head. The last thing he wanted was to be put on a mind altering chemical.

"Then I guess you have to live with the pain without any relief. I didn't want to go on any pills either but the pain was so bad I was forced to change my mind."

"I'm not going on any pills," Larry made clear.

"I can see Mr. Taylor is getting upset," Dr. Bellamy interrupted. "Does anyone else have any suggestions for Larry?"

"Maybe he could become a monk and withdraw from the world," the kid named Moe said in a flat tone of voice.

"That's enough, Moe. If no one else has any suggestions for Mr. Taylor, I'd like to open this meeting up for discussion. Who'd like to begin?"

"I think Stuart is doing drugs," Wayne told Dr. Bellamy.

"What!" Stuart's face turned red.

"You heard me. I think you're doing drugs," Wayne repeated.

"What gives you that idea?" Dr. Bellamy asked Wayne.

"I keep finding white powder on the bureau of the room we share. Somehow Stuart must be getting his buddies to bring him dope. If you ask me, the way they check out people coming in here sucks."

"How about it, Stuart? Is there any validity to what Wayne is saying?" Dr. Bellamy asked.

"Can a horse fly? Of course not! If you ask me Wayne is just a troublemaker and is trying to get attention." Stuart looked ready to explode. His face was as red as a beet and he seemed ready to punch Wayne out.

"Stuart-you need to calm down," Bellamy told him. "One of the reasons you're here has to do with substance abuse so I have to ask you. Are you or are you not sniffing drugs in your room?"

"I told you. The answer is no."

"I want to believe you, Stuart. But you've lied to me before. I believe the best thing would be for me to meet with you and Wayne personally. After I meet with Mr. Taylor, I'll see you both in my office. Before I end this meeting, does anyone else have something they want to say?"

"Do you know when my discharge date is?" Sheila asked in her usual shy way.

"Not for a while, Sheila," Dr. Bellamy told her. "This meeting is over. Larry, come with me."

Larry followed Bellamy into his office and they both sat down.

"How did your encounter with the detective go yesterday," Dr. Bellamy asked.

"Not too well. He actually seemed to think I had something to do with the murder."

"Why did he think that?"

"Because my boss Mr. Hillman told him Vicki didn't call me about winning the lottery. It's my word against Hillman's. Then there's the fact that there were no signs of a break in. He thinks Vicki let in whoever killed her. He's still investigating, so there's hope he uncovers the truth. He told me a Tony Whiting cashed in a ticket from Sunshine Convenience. That's where Vicki told me she purchased hers, so I told Detective Greene he should question Tony Whiting."

"I guess he took you seriously. When I caught the noon news this morning they said Tony Whiting was being questioned as to Vicki's murder and how he came to win the jackpot. But Greene doesn't expect much to come of it. As far as he's concerned, you're the only witness that Vicki possessed a winning MegaMoney ticket and even so you did not actually see this ticket. It's your word against Hillman's and Whiting's. This appears to be a complicated scenario and what really happened may not be known either temporarily or forever. You have to focus your energy on getting well."

"I have to focus my energy on making sure Vicki's killer is caught."

"How are you going to do that? The Boston Police are already on the case. Larry, you must focus on getting well. You're here for a reason. And unless the cops turn up something on you, you're to be released in twenty-eight days. That's not a long time from now. Are you still feeling suicidal?"

"No. Not anymore."

"What changed?"

"I had a visit from my mother. She convinced me I couldn't add to her pain. It would be hard for her if she had to lose me too."

"Will she be coming back to visit you?"

"Yes. Every chance she gets. Since I'm no longer feeling suicidal, does that mean I'm off the suicide watch?"

"Maybe in another week or so."

"Another week! Why so long."

"You're not going anywhere. I want to be certain the depression doesn't overwhelm you again. Your mother being a major part of your life and the fact you don't desire to hurt her are good signs. We'll wait a week and if you're still doing well and participating in all activities, I'll take you off the suicide watch. You'll still remain on the unit but no one will be watching over you twenty-four hours a day. Of course until the day you're discharged you will meet with me every day," Dr. Bellamy explained. "I do have a question. This morning in group, you were very hostile to the use of any medication. Why is that?"

"I don't know," Larry shrugged. "Maybe because no one is certain how a lot of these psyche medicines work and I'd rather not have any chemicals in my body if I can help it."

"I see. Fair enough. Perhaps you can overcome your loss without the use of meds. It might be harder though."

"Nothing could be harder than losing Vicki," Larry said. "I can still see her. Every time I close my eyes, I see her face. Every time I sleep, she's in my dreams."

"It's extremely hard losing someone who's close to you, someone you've shared your life with. You'll never get over it, though in time it might get easier to deal with."

"If Detective Greene could figure out exactly how her murder was carried out in such a short period of time and bring those responsible to justice, maybe then it would be easier to deal with."

"I agree. Until then, you have to take care of yourself. I'm glad your mother is able to be such a big part of your life."

"So am I. We were always close though. All this can't be easy for her."

"No, it can't be," Dr. Bellamy glanced at his watch. "I'll catch up with you at some point tomorrow. For today we have to end our session."

Larry rose to his feet and left Dr. Bellamy's office. He saw Wayne and Stuart go into it just as Mel caught up to him.

"There's an art class going on in the day room. It'll look good if you participate," Mel steered Larry in the direction of the day room.

"What exactly do they do in art class," Larry asked.

"Oh, lots of things. Today they're doing paint-by-numbers."

"Paint-by-numbers! I haven't done that since I was a kid," Larry said.

"Go on in," Mel tried to push Larry into the dayroom.

"I don't think so," Larry tried to elude Mel's grasp.

"What's going on out there?" a middle-aged woman wearing an apron called, noticing the commotion in the doorway.

"Nothing," Mel grinned. "I'm only trying to coax a new patient into joining your class. He's a little shy."

"Don't be shy," the woman yelled to Larry. "My name's Doreen. Come and join the class."

"Thanks a lot," Larry murmured to Mel.

Doreen was pleased at the new addition to her class. "What's your name?"

"Larry."

"Well don't just stand there. Come on in," Doreen walked up to Larry and ushered him into the room. Mel hung back, laughing.

"We only have two paint-by-number kits left, so you can paint either this kitten scene or this mountain scene." She held up the two boxes for Larry to consider.

"I'll take the mountain scene," Larry decided. His mind was refusing to take any of this seriously.

"Good choice," Doreen gave him a big smile. "Now why don't you pull up a chair to one of the tables and get started."

For the next half an hour Larry concentrated on painting mountains. He was just getting into it when Doreen announced the class was over. Doreen told Larry he could finish his project next week as he left.

Mel was waiting for Larry outside the day room. "Now that wasn't so bad, was it?"

Larry shrugged. "It gave me something to do."

"It's supposed to take your mind off your problems."

"I need a cigarette," Larry walked past Mel and headed to the smoking room.

"Wait!" Mel faithfully followed the patient he'd been assigned to watch. "Don't mind if I join you."

They both lit up and sat silently smoking their cigarettes.

Larry broke the silence. "How long have you been working here?"

"You really want to know."

Larry exhaled a smoke ring. "Yeah, I do."

"Fifteen long years."

"So tell me. How does one become a mental health worker?"

"For me, I started here doing anything and everything. I worked kitchen, cleaning and laundry. I got along good with most of the patients and Dr. Cooley, he was the chief psychiatrist at the time, asked me if I wanted to take a few college courses and train to be a mental health worker. It paid better and was way more easier, so that's what I became."

"Do you like working here?"

"I could think of worse places to be working. I get to meet a lot of interesting people-like you for instance. A part of me hopes I've made a positive difference in people's lives."

"You know, if someone ever told me I'd someday wind up in a mental hospital, I wouldn't believe him or her. Yet here I am. A part of me still thinks I'm going to wake up tomorrow and everything will be all right. Vicki will be by my side and everything will be just as it was before."

"It's hard what you're going through, no question about that."

A nurse opened the door to the smoking room. "Mr. Taylor. Your mother is here to see you."

They both left the room and went into the day room where Mrs. Taylor was waiting.

Larry greeted his mother with a hug while Mel watched on. "It's so good to see you, mom. I'm so glad you came. Let's sit down," he led her to one of the plastic chairs in the day room.

"I brought you a suitcase of clothes, pajamas and personal items. The nurse at the front desk said she'd put it in your room as soon as she goes through it."

"Goes through it?"

"I guess it's some sort of policy so nothing sharp or illegal such as drugs is brought in," Larry's mother Helen explained. "At least that's what the nurse told me."

Larry wondered if the policy was followed just some of the time. How else could Stuart be getting the drugs he was supposedly using?

"I've got to talk with you, son. On the noon news it was said you somehow think this Mr. Whiting cashed in the ticket Vicki was killed for? Is that correct?"

"Yes."

"I don't know if you know this, but Mr. Whiting is a very wealthy man. Extremely wealthy. I don't know if he'd have a motive."

"You can never have enough money," Larry reasoned. "There's something fishy about the whole thing."

I don't know how to say this. But . . . . but do you think maybe, possibly, Vicki might have been playing a joke on you that she hit the MegaMoney drawing?"

Larry groaned. "You're starting to sound like Detective Greene. He thinks there might not have been a ticket also."

"What if there wasn't? What if Tony really did win and Vicki's murder is some kind of robbery gone wrong or the work of a madman?"

"You should have heard Vicki's voice on the phone that day. There's no way she could have been joking or I imagined the whole thing. I know Mr. Hillman doesn't back me up but Vicki was just as shocked as I was about winning. Josh Hillman and Tony Whiting are not telling the truth because they have something to hide."

Before Mrs. Taylor left she gave Larry some change so he could buy cigarettes and make phone calls. The first people Larry called were Vicki's parents in Rhode Island. They weren't in but Larry left a message where he was and that he knew what they were going through. Next Larry called Detective Greene.

"Greene here. What do you want?"

Larry could tell the detective wasn't in the best of moods.

"This is Lawrence Taylor. I'm calling to find out how the investigation into the murder of my wife is going."

"We're working on it. As you know or may not know, I spoke with Tony Whiting today. Nice place he has. Nice girlfriend. I don't think he had anything to do with Vicki's murder, but of course we're looking into every lead at this time."

"Obviously you're not looking too hard or you would have come up with something. You know what I'm going to do? I'm going to hire a private investigator to look into all of this the minute I get out of here."

"That certainly is your right. One other thing. We checked out all the cab companies in the area and none of the drivers recalled having you as a fare. And the police who were at the scene at your house following the murder don't remember seeing you pull up in a cab."

"That's because the driver left me off at the beginning of the street."

"Maybe."

"What do you mean 'maybe'? You're trying to pin this murder on me, aren't you?"

"You seem to think that's what I'm trying to do."

"Whatever. Just keep me posted when and if you do find out anything."

"Will do," Detective Greene hung up the phone.

Larry deposited some more change into the pay phone and dialed a very familiar number.

"Ideal Advertising," a pleasant voice answered.

"Linda, put Josh Hillman on the phone."

"May I tell him who's calling?"

"You don't recognize my voice? It's Larry Taylor."

"Sorry, Larry. I'll put you through."

"Lawrence! How are you?" Mr. Hillman's gruff voice boomed into the telephone. "I've heard about what happened to you wife. That's really terrible. I hope they catch whoever did such an awful thing."

"I heard you lied to Detective Greene about Vicki's call saying she won the MegaMoney jackpot. I want to know why."

"Call? What are you talking about?"

"The call my wife put into my office saying she had a winning ticket. You were in the room when the call came and afterwards I mumbled to you I was leaving to take Vicki to Lottery Headquarters to cash in the ticket. I demand to know why that isn't what you told to Detective Greene."

"Lawrence, my boy. No wonder you're locked away. There was no such call. I merely told Detective Greene the truth. That you were being delusional in this regard."

"Damn it, Hillman. Because of you Greene thinks I might have had something to do with the crime. Are you lying because you had something to do with my wife being killed!"

"Now calm down, Larry. You're not thinking clearly. Your mind has let go. There was no call from Vicki claiming she won MegaMoney. That's something you made up, maybe to cover the crime you committed!"

"Fuck you, Hillman. You know what? You haven't heard the last from me. I don't know how but I will get to the bottom of this. You're lying because you and this Whiting character have something to hide!"

"I don't ever want you calling me again, understand. If you do I'll tell Greene that you're harassing me."

"Asshole. You ain't heard the last of me yet," Larry made clear. He was visibly shaken and trembling when he put down the phone.

Mel strode over to where Larry stood. "You OK?"

"Yeah," Larry said even though he wasn't. He had one more call he wanted to make. He wanted to confront Tony Whiting and let him know he would never give up his quest for justice. As Mel watched nearby, Larry called information to get Tony's number, only to be told it was unlisted.

CHAPTER FOURTEEN

K imberly Long had a hard time concentrating during her nursing shift. Larry Taylor accusing her Tony of having something to do with a murder was ludicrous. No matter what Mr. Taylor's mental condition, he had no right to be making these crazy accusations. Taylor had probably committed his wife's murder himself and was using Tony and this Hillman guy as scapegoats.

After she got through from work, Kim decided to drive down to Harborside to give Taylor a piece of her mind. She lied and told the registration desk she was Taylor's cousin and was led to the locked unit Larry was on. "He's in the smoking room. Follow this corridor to the last door to your left."

For a while Kim stood beside the smoking room door wondering if she really should barge in. She took a deep breath and opened the door. Two men were sitting inside puffing away at their cigarettes. They looked up as Kim entered.

"New here?" Mel asked sociably. "Pull up a seat. We've got plenty of smokes."

Larry couldn't get over how beautiful this dark-haired, very slender girl was. She was every bit as pretty as Vicki had been, only in a different way.

"I'm not a patient here. The reason I'm here is to see him," she pointed at Larry. He looked exactly like the picture of him she had seen in the Boston Globe recently.

"Him?" Mel was confused.

Larry was also. "Me?"

"Yes, you," Kim said angrily.

"Who are you?"

"My name's Kimberly Long and I've had it with you accusing my boyfriend Tony with your accusations. Detective Greene was over this morning talking to Tony, all because of you. It isn't right you're dragging innocent people into your delusions. Tony couldn't hurt a fly and never even heard of this Mr. Hillman. I want you to cut the crap and never bring up Tony's name again. If you do I'll make sure Tony sues you for libel and slander. I hate you for what you're putting me and Tony through. This is, I hope, the first and last time I lay eyes on you." With that, Kim turned around and left the smoking room. She had said what was on her mind and meant it when she said she never wanted to see Taylor ever again.

This time the call came when he was having sex with some cheap whore he had picked up from the Combat Zone.

"Who is it?" Luke screamed into the phone. He had been on the verge of an orgasm and was pissed at being interrupted.

"Mitchell wants you to call him. It's important."

"Right away," he hung up the phone and started to get dressed. This could be the call he'd been waiting for.

"Where are you going?" the whore put her arms around him.

"I got to go make a quick call outside. I'll be right back," he rubbed her breasts.

"I'll be waiting," she gave him a seductive look and poured herself another drink.

Luke jogged up to the bank of phones at the other end of the parking lot after leaving his motel cabin. Quickly he dialed Mitchell's private number. "Cobra," he gave his new password.

"Lucas. How good of you to call."

"What can I do for you?"

"A certain Mr. Taylor is beginning to irritate me. He's become like an itch I can't scratch."

"Want me to take care of him?"

"That would be good. He gets out of Harborside in about two weeks. I want him eliminated immediately after. Think you can handle it?"

"With one hand tied around my back. As soon as Taylor gets out of that hospital he's as good as dead."

"I'm counting on you, Lucas. Don't disappoint me. You know how I can be when I get angry. I'm even willing to pay you double if you get rid of this Taylor guy quickly."

"You got it," Luke promised. "I won't disappoint you."

"You better not."

"I won't," Luke gushed. He started to say something else but Mitchell had already hung up the phone. He couldn't help smiling. In two weeks Taylor was a dead man and he got to be paid double for his efforts. What a country!

"Nice going," Mel patted Larry on the back. "Dr. Bellamy just told me you're no longer on a suicide watch."

"What a relief. Finally I can go to the bathroom without someone watching me like I'm some sort of criminal or something."

"Now, Mr. Taylor. That constant surveillance was only for your own protection," Mel started to laugh.

Larry laughed along with Mel. "I have some more good news. Dr. Bellamy told me he'll be releasing me as soon as my twenty eight days are up."

"There's no real reason to keep you. You're obviously not suicidal anymore and don't appear to be a threat to others. Should you ever need us in the future, we'll be here for you."

"You know something, Mel? Don't tell Dr. Bellamy I told you this, but in a way I'm scared to leave here."

"That's normal. You've come to rely on us during your stay and now Dr. Bellamy and I won't be there for you."

"Plus what's there for me to go home to? I don't think I can live in the house Vicki and I shared anymore."

"You might want to consider other arrangements where to stay."

"I already have. I'm going to live with my mother in East Boston until I can decide what to do."

"That's a real good idea," Mel agreed.

Finally the big day came and Larry was about to be released from the mental hospital.

"Take care of yourself," Dr. Bellamy shook Larry's hand.

"I'll miss you," Mel told him. "Don't take this the wrong way, but I hope I never see you here again." He impulsively gave Larry a hug.

"Ready?" Larry's mother asked. She was sitting atop of Larry's packed suitcase.

"I'm ready," Larry said, struggling to control his emotions.

Helen Taylor stood up and Larry picked up his suitcase. A nurse opened the door to the locked unit and let them out. Freedom! For four weeks he had lived in the safety of that locked unit and now he was free. It was exhilarating yet at the same time frightening.

It was a cloudy day outside as they both walked to Helen's parked car.

"Looks like it might rain," Larry mentioned as he put the suitcase in the trunk of the car.

"I think I just felt a raindrop."

"Mom, I don't know if I adequately thanked you for allowing me to stay with you. There's no way I could make it through all this if not for you. You mean the world to me."

"I'll always be there for you. That's something you can count on."

Luke sat in his parked car at the other end of the Harborside parking lot. He saw Taylor exit with an older woman who he assumed was probably his mother. He saw them both get into a red car and drive away. Maintaining a reasonable distance, Luke pulled out right after them and followed the car. Soon the car Taylor was in pulled into the driveway of an attractive single family home in East Boston. Larry and his mother got out of the car and retrieved the suitcase from the trunk. Then they both went inside the house.

Luke yawned. This was going to be easy. The first chance he got BINGO! he'd shoot Larry right between the eyes. Getting comfortable, he opened up a can of beer and settled down to wait until Taylor exited the house.

"Are you hungry?" Mrs. Taylor asked once she and Larry were inside the house.

"I'm fine, mom," Larry answered, putting down the suitcase.

"Are you sure? At least let me make you a cup of tea."

"Really, I don't want anything. Can I see the yellow pages?"

"Yellow pages? What do you need the yellow pages for?"

"I want to see if I can find a private investigator to look into Vicki's murder. It's been a month now and the police still haven't discovered anything."

"The yellow pages are in the kitchen by the phone. But do you really think a private detective can do better than the Boston Police?"

"I don't know. All I know is that Vicki was murdered for her MegaMoney ticket and the police are not taking me theory very seriously. Hiring a private investigator is all I can think of to do."

Suddenly a booming noise shook the house and rattled all the windows.

"Thunder," Mrs. Taylor stated as huge raindrops fell against the house. She walked over and closed the kitchen windows.

Larry took a seat by the phone and started skimming through the yellow pages under private investigators. There were numerous listings but a display ad caught his eye. Need a detective? it said. As a matter of fact, I do, Larry dialed the number listed below the advertisement.

"Rolando Torres speaking," a man with a heavy Spanish accent picked up the phone. "How can I help you?"

"My name is Lawrence Taylor. You might have heard my name recently in the media. My wife was murdered a month ago."

"Yes, of course I did. You're the guy claiming his wife was killed for a lottery ticket."

"I was wondering if I could come by and speak with you. I saw your ad in the yellow pages and am wondering if it is worth my while to hire a private investigator."

"When would you like to come by? I have some time now if you're not doing anything. I'm located on 200 State

Street, right by the Boston Harbor and near South Station. Think you can find me? If now isn't convenient, next time I could see you would be a week from Monday."

"No. Right now is fine. I really want to talk to someone about all this as soon as possible."

"How fast can you get here?"

"Give me a half an hour."

"Great. Just buzz my office when you get in the lobby. It's after five, so most people have left for the day and the building is closed. I'll come down and let you in. I'm on the third floor under Torres."

"I'm on my way," Larry hung up the phone.

His mother noticed Larry seemed ready to go out. "It's raining really heavily out there. Maybe you should wait to see if it lets up a little."

"I can't. I told Mr. Torres I'd be there in half an hour."

"I don't like you going out in such a storm."

"Can I borrow your car, mom?"

"You know you can. I just want you to be careful. There's a lot of thunder and lightening with this storm."

"I'll be fine," Larry gave his mother a kiss and was almost out the front door when his mother called him back. In her hand was a yellow large size rain jacket.

"This used to be your father's when he was alive. I still wear it sometimes when the weather is bad. I want you to put it on. I'm not going to let you leave the house until you do. You don't need a cold on top of everything else."

That ugly thing, Larry was tempted to say, but he put it on. Between his mother's bright purple car and his neon yellow rain jacket, he'd really stand out.

"I'm going to make a late dinner that will be ready when you come back," Helen told him. "So come straight home afterwards. Good luck meeting with this detective."

"Thanks," Larry rushed out of the house. It was raining cats and dogs and Larry put up the hood of the raincoat and pulled it tight as he rushed towards his mother's car. His feet were soaking wet from stepping in all the puddles. He fumbled for the key when he finally reached the car and let himself in. He hoped Rolando Torres would wait if he were a few minutes late.

Luke was on his seventh beer can when he saw Taylor leave the house. Even through the sheets of heavy rain there was no missing the bright yellow raincoat Taylor had chosen to wear. The minute Larry pulled out of the parking spot, Luke began to follow him.

Completely unaware he was being followed, Larry Taylor was in deep thought as he drove towards the South Station area. He had to drive slowly and carefully because of the weather and it took him another fifteen minutes until he located 200 State Street. The parking lot of 200 State Street was vacant so Larry was able to pretty much park by the front door. The rain was still coming down buckets as he darted from his car into the office lobby. He looked up Torres in the building directory and pressed the corresponding buzzer. Then he waited for Torres to come downstairs and let him in.

Luke pulled his car up directly in front of Larry's. Through his window he could see Taylor anxiously standing inside the building's small lobby. Should he get out of the car and go shoot Taylor right now? Too late. Someone had opened the main door and Taylor disappeared inside.

"Shit," Luke cursed. He had blown that opportunity. But Taylor had to come out sometime and Luke would be waiting for him.

"Sorry I'm late," Larry apologized to Torres.

"Don't mention it," Torres smiled and shook Larry's hand. "This is a real old building and there is no elevator. We'll have to take the stairs to my office."

Larry followed Torres up to a cluttered, tiny office on the third floor. Rolando took some papers from a chair and Larry sat down.

"Tell me your story," Torres sat down behind an equally cluttered desk.

"Well, on June 18th I was at work at Ideal Advertising. My boss, Mr. Josh Hillman was in my office going over some project with me when the phone to my direct line rang. It was my wife Vicki. She was totally hysterical that she had won the MegaMoney drawing. Actually, she was one of two winners, so she and the other winner would each get half of a hundred million jackpot. Anyway, I assured her I'd be right home. Vicki wanted to go to Lottery Headquarters right away to cash in her ticket. But when I got to my car it had a flat. I took a cab home and there were a lot of police on my street. When I went inside I found out Vicki had been murdered."

"That's when you tried to commit suicide?"

"Correct. I couldn't take it. I saw no life for myself without Vicki. When I was at Harborside a Detective Greene came to interview me. He told my one of the tickets cashed in had been bought at Sunshine Convenience. That's when I recalled Vicki had said she purchased hers there. Tony Whiting cashed in the ticket purchased there.

So in a nutshell, my theory is somehow Hillman tipped off Whiting or whoever to go kill my wife and get the ticket. Then Whiting cashes it in."

"Wow. That's quite a theory. Have the police talked to Hillman?"

Larry sighed. "Yes. But he denies my wife ever called that day. That, the fact no one other than Vicki ever saw the ticket in her possession and that there was no break in have the police wondering if I might have committed the crime. They won't come out and say so yet, at least in so many words, but I know that's what they're thinking."

Rolando Torres leaned back in his chair. "This is a fascinating chain of events. Truthfully, I don't know how much I'll be able to help you. But tell you what. I'll poke around a bit, interview some people myself, like the people that work at this Sunshine Convenience. I won't charge you unless I uncover anything useful. Does that sound OK?"

"That sounds great," Larry said with relief. "I hope you're able to uncover clues the police might have missed."

"So do I," Torres got up from his chair. He had Larry write his phone number on a piece of paper so he could get in touch with him later. "You're not going to believe this," Torres walked over to a small closet and pulled a yellow rain jacket. "This is the same brand rain jacket you walked in here with. We must have the same taste."

"Actually, the one I had on once belonged to my dad."

"What happened to him?"

"Sudden heart attack when I was young."

"Tragic," Rolando shook his head. "I just lost my dad recently." He put on his rain jacket as Larry put on his. "You better put the hood on too," he told Larry. "It still might be raining hard out there.

Standing side by side with Rolando, with their hoods on, Larry thought they could pass as brothers. They both left the office and Rolando locked the door with a special key.

"Ready to face the rain?" Torres said as he and Larry walked downstairs.

"Actually, I'd like to use the men's room," Larry admitted. "Is there one that's open?"

When they got to the first floor Torres pointed to a door some distance down a dark hallway. "I'll be right out," Larry promised.

"I'll wait for you outside," Rolando told him. "I want to see if the rain has let up any."

"OK," Larry headed towards the men's room.

Luke sat patiently in his car waiting for Larry to walking out that front door. He looked forward to all that money Mitchell was going to pay him for this hit. No question about it. He was one fellow who loved his job.

Suddenly his heart beat faster. Someone had just stepped out the front door of the office building and that somebody was wearing an ugly yellow rain jacket. This was Luke's chance.

He opened the door to his car and leaned out. "Mr. Taylor," he called. The man with the raincoat on looked up.

That's when Luke shot him, right between the eyes like he said he would. The man went down and his hood blew off his head. Then he collapsed in a dead heap.

Luke walked over to the body. Something wasn't quite right. He realized this man's face was different and he wasn't quite as tall as Taylor, or nearly as thin. Damn it! He had shot impulsively and killed the wrong man. How was he to know another individual with an exact yellow rain coat was going to exit the same building Taylor had just went into? Mitchell wasn't going to like it. But wait! Taylor had still to exit and this time he'd be ready for him.

Larry left the bathroom and walked out of the lobby of 200 State Street. It was still raining outside, but not as much as it had been earlier. He pulled his hood off and unbuttoned his raincoat. Where was Rolando? He looked around and then he spotted a person wearing a yellow rain jacket lying on the ground. "Mr. Torres!" Larry yelled, running up to the body. There was blood all over Rolando's face and Larry realized Torres had been shot and killed.

Before Larry had time to react further, something whizzed by him and clanked against one of the garbage cans standing by the side of the building. Someone was shooting at him! He was now the target of whoever had shot Rolando.

With lightening speed Larry took off running. His only hope was to out distance his assailant.

"Fuck!" Luke cursed, hurrying after his target as Larry ran towards the warehouse district of Boston Harbor. How could he have missed shooting Larry when the man had been right in front of him? This was the first time anything like this had ever happened. His aim was always perfect.

Oh well, no use crying over spilled milk. The warehouse district was deserted this time of night and Luke was a fast runner. There was no way he was going to let Taylor get away.

Larry could hear the steady beat of footsteps pounding the pavement right behind him. Again he felt something whiz by and realized he had to do something or he would be killed just like Rolando.

The streets of the warehouse district were like a ghost town. There was absolutely no one around but Larry. And a cold-blooded killer.

CRASH! Larry's ankle gave out and he fell to the ground. He had tripped over what was either a large rock or a brick. The pain in his ankle was excruciating. He wouldn't be able to run very fast or far on it. He had to think of something quickly or else he wasn't going to get out of this alive.

Climbing to his feet, Larry ran as fast as he could to the Boston Harbor side of the warehouse district. There was one escape, if he lived through it.

The closer he came to the water, the more he could hear the frigid waters splashing against the docks of the warehouses. He ran to the edge of one of the docks, said a prayer, and jumped.

The chilly waters of the Atlantic Ocean momentarily shattered his senses. Down, down, down he went, wondering if he was going to drown. Gradually his descent into the murky water slowed, but he became confused. Which way was up? He had no idea. Shock and panic began to set in. The pressure in his lungs made them feel like they were going to burst. Which way was up?

Just as he felt he would surely pass out his head broke through the surface of the dirty water. Larry gasped for air, taking in huge mouthfuls of salty water. He was alive.

Maybe not for long. Larry looked up and could see the man who had been shooting at him standing on the dock. The rain had subsided and Larry could clearly see the gun in the man's hand. Pointing at Larry's head, the man fired into the water.

The shot missed, and the water around Larry broke out into countless tiny ripples. The man stood at the edge of the dock, waiting for Larry to exit the freezing cold water. Every now and then, he would fire a shot in the direction of Larry's head.

Larry was becoming extremely tired. He couldn't last in this frigid water much longer. The Logan Airport side of the harbor was a long way off, but he had to try to swim to it. Otherwise he'd drown and this hit man would succeed in his mission to kill him after all.

Larry began to swim towards Logan Airport. It was his only hope. He really figured he could make that far.

Somehow he miscalculated. The airport had looked closer than it really was. Glancing back, Larry could still see the shooter hanging out on the warehouse dock.

His lips started turning blue and he felt like he was about to lose consciousness. So this is how his life ended. Drowning between Logan Airport and South Station.

It seemed to come out of nowhere, a small boat plowing through the turbulent water. Larry could hear it before he even saw it. "Over here!" he began shouting, hoping they would hear. "Help!"

Slowly, at what seemed like an eternity, the boat began to turn and come his way.

"Over here!" Larry urged it on. He started waving his arms, hoping the boat would see him in the dark. "Hurry. I can't stay afloat much longer."

The boat got closer and two pairs of strong arms helped Larry aboard. Exhausted, Larry collapsed on the deck. It was only then that he noticed several people sitting on wooden chairs inside the craft. A lot of them were wearing business suits.

"Relax," one of the men who had pulled him aboard told Larry. "You're on the South Station to Logan Airport water taxi. You are mighty lucky indeed. This is our last trip to Logan for the night. How is it you find yourself in the middle of Boston Harbor on such a stormy night?"

Larry shivered against the cold night air. He slumped into one of the hard wooden chairs, too exhausted to speak.

"You don't have to talk," the crewman said. "I've radioed for an ambulance. It'll be waiting for us the minute we pull up at Logan. You can tell them and the people at the hospital what happened."

Larry nodded, much too tired to think or respond.

CHAPTER FIFTEEN

"You say somebody was chasing you?" an emergency medical technician asked Larry as they rode in the ambulance on the way to the hospital.

"Yes. He was also shooting at me," Larry said as he shivered underneath a wool blanket he was wrapped in. "One man is dead already. I saw the body. That's why I jumped into the Boston harbor. To get away."

"Someone from the police department is meeting us at County Hospital. He or she would be very interested in what you have to say. Meantime, try to relax. We'll be at County within the next fifteen minutes."

"Mr. Taylor," Detective Greene paced the small room on the medical floor where Larry lay. "Tell me again the events which transpired tonight."

"As I told you I was going to do, I consulted with a private investigator earlier. His name is Rolando Torres and he has an office at 200 State Street. Or should I say had an office at 200 State. After I consulted with him, Mr. Torres stepped outside while I went to use the men's room. When I finally went outside, I saw Mr. Torres lying on the ground. He had been shot and was dead."

"Any idea who might have shot him?"

"I have a theory. Let me finish. As I approached Torres' body, someone shot at me. I started to run and the shooter ran after me. I twisted my ankle and knew then I couldn't out distance whoever was after me, so I took a chance and jumped into the harbor. I started to swim towards Logan Airport when I realized I would not make it. That water taxi coming when it did saved my life. Now to get back to my theory. Whoever shot Torres meant to shoot me. We were both wearing a yellow raincoats and the shooter must have gotten us mixed up."

"Why would someone be after you?"

"Because I'm the only one who knows my wife called me saying she won MegaMoney. I'm implicating Hillman and Whiting. Either one of them could want me out of the way."

"We'll be sending a car to 200 State Street. They'll be radioing me as soon as a body is found."

"His body is a little to the left as you walk into the main entrance. They can't miss it."

"They'll search the whole area. I'll be by as soon as I hear something."

Detective Greene was back within thirty minutes, a hot cup of coffee in his hand.

"Did they find the body?" Larry questioned, sitting up in bed.

"There was no body. Zippo."

"What do you mean there was no body? It was there! I saw it with my own eyes,"

"Like I said, there was no body. However, that doesn't mean nothing happened. A bullet was recovered from one of the garbage cans near the building."

"I'm telling you. There was a body. This shooter must have gone back and disposed of it."

Detective Greene gave Larry a meaningful look. "That's not all. The bullet we recovered was from the same type of gun used to shoot Mrs. Taylor."

"So my theory is correct. The same person who murdered my wife is now trying to eliminate me."

"That is one theory. Mr. Taylor, do you own a gun?"

"I told you no and I don't like being asked again."

"Your evening in our pristine harbor. Could it have been another suicide attempt?"

"Absolutely not. I'm telling you. A murder happened at 200 State Street tonight and I was nearly a victim myself. I'm sick and tired of you not taking me seriously."

"A funny thing about bodies, Mr. Taylor. They have a way of popping up and leading us directly to the killer. If this Torres guy has been murdered, we'll find him. Meantime, we're going to put a missing person's bulletin out on him. One way or another, we'll find this Torres person. If a murder did happen tonight, I only hope this Torres body doesn't point to you being the murderer."

"You idiot!" Mitchell was screaming loudly. "You absolute idiot! What do you mean you killed the wrong man!"

"It was raining," Luke explained. "How would I know someone else would be wearing the same ugly raincoat identical to Taylor's? He came out of the same building Taylor went into."

"You mindless retard!" Mitchell was seething. "I didn't know you based your hits on what the subject is wearing!"

"It was a honest mistake," Luke cowered. He hated it when Mitchell was angry. "You know I've never screwed up on you before."

"That's the only thing saving you by a thread. Jesus! You shot the wrong guy! How could you be so stupid?"

"I went after Taylor when he finally exited the building but he pulled a fast one on me. He jumped into Boston Harbor and would have drowned if that stupid water taxi hadn't picked him up."

"Great. So other then getting wet behind the ears, the man is still alive."

"I went back and disposed of the dead man's body by dumping it in some woods off of Cape Cod. I'm calling you from the Cape right now."

"Whatever. I want this Taylor guy taken care of and I want it done soon. How can I ever trust you again?"

"Does lightening strike the same tree twice? I won't goof up this time. I promise."

"I don't know? Maybe I should get someone else to take care of the Taylor problem?"

"Don't even think of it. I'll get this Taylor guy if it's the last thing I ever do."

"OK, Lucas. I'm going to give you one last chance. Fuck up this time and don't expect me to ever hire you again."

"Don't worry about a thing. I've learned my lesson. Absolutely no more mistakes. When I make my move the only thing Lawrence Taylor will be good for is dog meat."

Kimberly Long could not believe it. Her nursing supervisor had the nerve to assign Lawrence Taylor to her as a patient! When Kim had complained she was told her job was to treat anyone who was a patient on her medical unit. Still, she was fascinated. The report said Taylor was barely alive in the middle of Boston Harbor when a Logan Airport water taxi had saved him. Probably trying to kill himself again, Kim reasoned. Out of all the hospitals in the Boston area, why did Larry have to wind up in this one?

Slowly, not wanting to, she walked into the room on her unit where Taylor had been brought for observation. "Remember me?" she asked, trying to control her anger. Even if Taylor was crazy, he had no right to accuse Tony of a murder conspiracy regarding his winning the MegaMoney drawing.

Larry looked up. He was still good and cold from his battle with the Atlantic Ocean, a battle the ocean had nearly won. "From the mental hospital. You're the girlfriend of the man who murdered, or had someone else murder, my wife for the winning MegaMoney ticket. I didn't know you were a nurse?"

Kim felt like slapping Larry for that remark regarding Tony, but knew she couldn't. "Yes, I'm a nurse." Luckily Larry would not be on this floor for too long.

"Do you know why I am here? Because someone now is trying to kill me. I didn't just decide to take a dunk in Boston Harbor on a stormy night. Someone was shooting at me. This someone had already killed a man he thought was me and nearly succeeded in getting rid of me too."

"I'm sure you told the police all this?" Kim did not know whether to take him seriously or not. Did someone really shoot at Taylor or was he just saying that?

"Of course I did, Kim. Do you mind if I call you Kim?"

She did mind, but for some reason said no.

"I'm telling you, Kim. Someone is after me. If you could have seen how determined this killer was chasing me through the warehouse district. It was as if he were a professional. I had never been so scared in my entire life. I'm sure your boyfriend Tony has something to do with this."

"Stop," Kim said firmly. "I'll put up with you saying anything else, just don't go dragging Tony's name into all this. He's a fine, decent man and I won't have you go slandering him in this way with your delusions. You want to know what I think? I think you're still suicidal. A lot of depressed people try to end their lives several times before they succeed. And that's what I'm going to treat you as. As a depressed individual who can't come to terms with the death of his wife. A death, by the way, that he was responsible for," Kim let slip by before she could stop herself.

"Fuck you."

"The feeling is mutual, let me assure you," Kim said. "You look fine to me, so I think I'll be going. I have more important things to take care of."

"Don't let me stop you," Larry called as Kim left the room.

Luckily, the rest of Kim's shift passed without incidence. She stayed far away as possible from the room Lawrence Taylor was assigned to, not trusting herself to confront him again. Finally, her tiring shift ended and it was time to go home.

"You'll never guess who was a patient on my floor tonight," she asked Tony the second she got home.

"Would it be a certain Mr. Taylor?"

"The one and only."

"The news ran a story on his rescue from Boston Harbor. It's not every day someone gets plucked out of the middle of our harbor, alive at that."

"You know, I can't figure this Mr. Taylor out. He still insists you had something to do with his wife's murder, allegedly for the MegaMoney ticket that you cashed in. Isn't there anything you can do? Like sue him for slander or something like that? He shouldn't be allowed to go around making wild accusations against innocent people without the slightest shred of evidence."

"I've thought about it, but I'd rather not get involved in legal action against a crazy individual. Mr. Taylor is delusional and paranoid person. I'm sure that's the way others see him."

"I think he could have murdered his wife himself," Kim sat down on Tony's lap.

Tony stroked her long, dark hair. "That's a good possibility. I'm confident all this will blow over soon. Mr. Taylor is under a lot of stress. It's only a matter of time before he cracks and winds up in a mental institution again, or like you said, is found guilty of killing his wife."

Why wasn't his sleeping pill working? Larry wanted to know. He tossed and turned and turned and tossed until he could take no more of it. He rang for a nurse.

"Yes," an unsympathetic, overweight figure eventually came into his room. At least it wasn't that Kim Long woman.

"I need another sleeping pill," Larry demanded.

"You just got one forty minutes ago," the male nurse growled.

"I don't care. I need another one right now."

"Do you realize I'm going to have to wake some poor, overworked doctor in the middle of the night for the sole reason of getting you another sleeping pill? Don't you feel guilty?"

"I don't care what you have to do. I want another sleeping pill. I feel terrible and am having trouble sleeping because I'm still freezing cold. If you won't call the doctor, I demand to speak with a supervisor."

"I'll see what I can do," the man strode out of the room. He returned thirty minutes later with a single Dalmane in a small, paper cup.

"Thanks," Larry said, gulping it down. Somehow he managed to fall into a restless, troubled sleep.

In the morning when he woke up his mother was standing by his bed.

"Hi, mom," Larry said weakly.

"You have no idea how worried I was about you," Mrs. Taylor said seriously. "How are you?"

"A lot better than last night," Larry answered. That freezing cold feeling was all but gone. "I'm sorry I made you worry."

"The main thing is you're all right. What happened? The story of your rescue from Boston Harbor was on the news, but they didn't give specifics."

"I met with that detective I told you yesterday evening I was going to meet with. He had a yellow raincoat just like mine. He stepped outside while I went to use the restroom. When I exited the building I found him laying on the ground. He had been shot in the face and there wasn't much left. Then someone started shooting at me. I started running as fast as I could. Suddenly I tripped and twisted my ankle. I knew I couldn't out run the shooter so I had no choice but to jump into Boston Harbor to get away. But this guy wouldn't leave. He kept shooting into the water and waiting for me to come out. I was becoming numb and semi-conscious from the cold, so I decided to swim to the other side, to Logan Airport. I couldn't make it though, and would have drowned if the South Station to Logan Airport water taxi hadn't picked me up."

"I was so concerned, thinking this might have been another suicide attempt.

But someone out to get you, that's really scary."

"Breakfast," a young girl with a hair net on brought in a tray for Larry.

"I'm not hungry," Larry pushed it aside.

"Who's not hungry?" a deep voice asked. In the doorway stood a bulky man with a long white lab coat on and a stethoscope hanging around his neck. "I'm Dr. Christopher. Dr. Adams briefed my on your case yesterday and upon my review of your lab reports and x-rays, I'd say everything looks pretty much normal. Given this fact, we'll be discharging you this afternoon."

"So soon?" Mrs. Taylor asked.

"There's no reason to keep him here. However, I did ask Dr. Mable, our resident psychiatrist to meet with Mr. Taylor before he's discharged."

"No," Larry said firmly.

"Mr. Taylor. You've been under a lot of stress and it only best you get to the bottom of it and remain under the care of a professional."

"No way. I've had enough of psychiatry. They'll never bring Vicki back and I refuse to meet with this guy."

"Perhaps it's not such a bad idea," Larry's mother spoke up. "I only want what's best for you, Larry."

"I'm not meeting with a psychiatrist."

"Very well, then," Dr. Christopher turned to leave. "One of the nurses will be bringing you discharge papers to sign right after lunch. From that point on, you're free to leave."

"OK," Larry agreed. When Dr. Christopher left, he changed into some street clothes his mother had brought him.

"Maybe you should have agreed to see Dr. Mable," Mrs. Taylor nervously suggested.

"No. I'm not seeing another psychiatrist. I know you're concerned, but trust me, I'm not delusional and did not try to commit suicide last night. Someone was shooting at me and that's how I wound up in the middle of Boston Harbor. You do believe me, don't you, mom?"

"You're my son, of course I believe you. When you come home, we'll figure out what to do next."

Luckily, when Kim arrived to work earlier, Lawrence Taylor had already been discharged, so she did not have to deal with him. But she did have to deal with what felt like a bad cold coming on. Sniffling and sneezing, she could barely concentrate on her job. So when the nursing supervisor suggested she take the rest of the evening off, Kim did not resist. She rushed home with thoughts of chicken soup to sip while laying in a nice, warm bed.

Opening the door to her penthouse suite apartment, she realized Tony was not alone. She heard voices coming from the library. Giving Tony some privacy, she went into the kitchen and heated up some chicken soup. She was about to take it to the bedroom she and Tony shared when the door to the library opened up.

"Kim. I didn't hear you come in," Tony said shakily.

"I wasn't feeling well."

"Sorry to hear that," Tony stammered. It was clear he was not expecting Kim to arrive home before her shift ended. "Let me just show this man out the door."

Kim took a hard look at the gentleman standing next to Tony. She had seen him someplace before but could not place it.

"Who was that?" Kim asked when they were alone.

"Just a friend," Tony answered evasively.

"I thought he looked rather familiar."

"I can't imagine why. His name is Roger Hardy. I'm sure you haven't met him before."

"Probably not," Kim pretended to drop the subject. "I really could use some cold medicine. Would you mind going to drugstore at Copley Place for me?"

"I'd be happy to," Tony said. He seemed grateful Kim had dropped the subject.

A few minutes after Tony had gone, Kim took the elevator down to the Prudential lobby. Anyone going to the above apartments had to sign in and show an ID She was certain she had seen Tony's friend somewhere before.

She asked to security guard to show her who had signed in to visit the apartments today. He handed her a heavy, thick book. It didn't take Kim long to see who the last person was who had signed in to visit the penthouse suite. She had seen his picture in the paper recently. It was the other man Larry had accused of plotting to kill his wife. Mr. Josh Hillman had just been visiting Tony Whiting.

"Why did you lie to me?" Kim asked Tony when her returned home with her cold medicine.

"What do you mean?" Tony took off his coat.

"About Roger Hardy. That wasn't Roger Hardy that was just here. That was Josh Hillman. You told the police you didn't know him."

"I didn't tell you the truth because I did not want to worry you. You see, Mr. Hillman is considering some legal action against Taylor's accusations and wished to speak to me to see if I was with him on this. That's all there is to it."

Kim bit her lip. Tony's explanation certainly sounded reasonable. She decided just to forget the whole thing for now and go and get some rest.

CHAPTER SIXTEEN

"I feel so nervous," Mrs. Taylor declared as she paced the interior of her living room while Larry lay on the sofa. "To think, someone might be actually after you. Larry, I'm scared."

"I know how you feel," Larry agreed.

"You need to get out of here," Helen advised. "I've been thinking about that a lot.

I have friends in New York City. Perhaps you should go there?"

"I don't want to put anyone in any danger."

"You wouldn't have to stay with them. But I think it's a good idea for you to get far away from Boston."

"I don't think the police would be too happy if I were to suddenly pack up and leave. However, you're right. I need to get away from here. New York City sounds like a good place as any to try to lose myself."

"You look tired. Why don't you get some rest? While dinner is in the oven, I'll get on the phone to Amtrak to get you a ticket for tomorrow to New York."

"I really appreciate it. I don't know what I'd do without you," Larry said. In a few minutes he was asleep.

The next thing he knew, his mother was waking him up.

"Huh?" Larry rubbed the sleep from his eyes. For a moment he was confused, thinking he was still at County Hospital. He got up and joined his mother for a roast beef dinner.

"You were asleep for over two hours," his mother informed him. "It broke my heart to wake you, but I didn't want the food to become cold."

"No. You were right to wake me. I'm starving," Larry helped himself to some mashed potatoes.

"Let me tell you what I did while the meat was in the oven. I remembered there was these big trunks in the attic filled with your old baby items and pictures. There's really quite a lot of stuff up there. Remember your old stuffed brown bear you named Snuggles? He's up there."

"Really? You hung on to him for so many years? Of course I remember Snuggles. When we finish, I want to go up to the attic to see these pictures and items myself."

"I also called Amtrak. You have a train to New York to catch tomorrow at two in the afternoon. The ticket is under the name Micheal Bolling and you can pick it up at the reservation desk."

Larry was impressed. "You think of everything."

"I try to," Helen said modestly.

After dinner, Larry offered to clear the table and do the dishes. He cut himself another piece of apple pie before putting the tin in the refrigerator and joined his mother in the living room. "Is it OK if I go up to the attic now and look through all my childhood things?"

"Of course. I'd join you but it is after ten at night and I want to get ready for bed."

"I want to stay up there and look through everything, so I guess I'll say good night now. I'll see you for breakfast," Larry gave his mother a kiss.

"Don't stay up there too long. You've got a train to New York to catch tomorrow."

"I won't," Larry promised.

He finished his pie and climbed the stairs to the attic. It was dusty and warm up there and he sneezed several times. Finally he found the light switch and turned it on. Inside the attic stood two trunks and other odd junk. His mother said his pictures and baby stuff were in the trunks, so that's where he started. True enough, the photos were charming. There he was on his first day of school. First time riding a bicycle. First time on the beach. And there was Snuggles! He hadn't seen his old friend in decades. Snuggles was all-time favorite stuffed animal. How many sleepless nights in his younger years had he laid awake in bed with only Snuggles to keep him company? Perhaps needing a security blanket for comfort, he even debated taking Snuggles with him to New York City before shooting down that plan. For decades Snuggles had remained safe and sound right here in his mother's attic and that's where he would remain.

Boy was it ever warm. Larry was becoming drowsy from the heat. If only for a second, he rested his head against Snuggles and the trunk. Without meaning to, he fell asleep.

Luke grinned. He had seen Larry eating dinner with his mother earlier and then the whole house had gone dark. Except for the attic light. It had been on for hours and Luke was beginning to think they had just forgotten to shut if off. That was probably it.

He checked his watch. Three a.m. Perfect. No one was is sight as he got out of his car and approached the Taylor residence. In his hand was a heavy one-gallon container filled with gasoline. He walked around the building slowly, pouring some of the precious fluid as he went. When he had circled the entire residence, he lit a match and dropped it to the ground.

Only when the fire was going good and strong did he flee the scene.

It was a sweltering hot day and Larry was driving his car along Storrow Drive. He turned on the air conditioner but for some reason it wasn't working. He pressed the button to lower the driver's side window but nothing happened. By this time he was perspiring heavily, so much so that he pulled the car over to the breakdown lane and parked. He had to get some fresh air soon or he'd sweat to death. The car was like an inferno, becoming hotter and hotter with each second. Panic set in as he tried all the car windows and doors to escape. It was almost as if someone had glued the vehicle shut. If he didn't get help soon, he was going to die right here in the breakdown lane of Boston's Storrow Drive. In desperation, he leaned against the horn, hoping, praying someone would come get him out of this car before it was too late ...

With a jolt, Larry woke up, his heart pounding in his chest. Where was he? Now he remembered. He must have fallen asleep while looking through the trunkfuls of baby stuff in his mother's attic. It had been many years since he had a nightmare. But what was that horn-like noise? In his dream he was leaning against the car's horn, but now he was awake and he could still hear it. In fact, it sounded almost like a fire alarm.

Fire Alarm! Instantly Larry jumped to his feet. The fire alarm was going off and he was trapped in the attic. Smoke was already seeping through the door to the attic door and flames were coming through the floor. There didn't look like anything he could do except sit back and await death. If only there was a window he could break down . . .

There was! The skylight window. He had completely forgotten about it.

Larry dragged one of the heavy trunks until it was directly below the skylight window. With considerable effort, he lifted the other trunk and placed on top of the first one. Grabbing a pair of old skis which were in a corner, Larry climbed on top of this mini tower of two trunks. Using the skis, he smashed through the skylight window. Shards of broken glass rained down on him but he didn't stop until all the glass had been smashed and none remained in the window. Cool, welcoming air rushed in through the opening.

There was no time to lose. It took several tries, but somehow he managed to haul himself through the opening and on to the roof. From what he could see, the whole house was engulfed in flames and parts of the roof were no exception.

The only thing he could do was jump of the roof and hope he didn't break any bones or worse. A thundering boom shook the house and a portion of the roof next to him collapsed. Taking a deep breath, Larry said a mental prayer and jumped off the edge of the roof into nothingness.

Every inch of his body hurt like hell. How long he had been unconscious for he did not know.

"You're a very lucky man," a nurse looking down at him smiled.

A nurse. He had to be in a hospital of some kind. Suddenly it all came back to him. The fire. His escape from the attic through the skylight window. The jump off the roof into nothingness.

"It's a good thing you landed in some bushes," a masculine voice spoke up. "Otherwise you might not have fared so well."

Painfully, Larry turned his head in the direction of the man's head. It was Dr. Christopher and it could only mean one thing. He was a patient again on County's inpatient medical unit.

A powerful concern blocked all his thoughts. He had to know. "My mother. Is she in this hospital too? How is she?"

Dr. Christopher and the nurse fidgeted. Finally Dr. Christopher cleared his throat. "Mr. Taylor. I'm afraid I have some very bad news for you."

"Tell me! Did my mother make it out of the fire or not!"

"I'm afraid not," Dr. Christopher informed Larry.

"No," Larry started crying. He was losing anyone and everyone who ever meant anything to him.

"There's a Detective Greene from the Boston Police waiting in the hallway to see you. I can tell him this isn't a good time," Dr. Christopher suggested.

"It's OK," Larry dried his eyes. He wanted to hear what Detective Greene made of this.

"Well, well, well," Robert Greene strode into the room. "Back at County again. All kidding aside though. I am sorry you lost your mother in last night's fire."

"Right. As if you care."

"I do care. Really."

"Sure. You're probably going to accuse me of setting the fire."

"Actually, there are a lot of unanswered questions. The fire was definitely arson. No question about that."

"So you're thinking I happened to set it just as I happened to jump into Boston Harbor the night before."

"You seem certain I'm out to implicate you."

"Aren't you?"

"Truthfully, I have no concrete theories or evidence on anything at the moment, even though this fire could have been yet another suicide gone wrong."

"See-you are thinking I'm behind everything."

"I'd be a fool not to look at every possibility. We're working day and night to uncover who killed your wife, your mother and potentially that detective you consulted. All I can do is reassure you we're determined to get to the bottom of all this."

"Soon, I hope. I can't take much more of this." Memories of his mother flooded Larry's mind. Memories of her baking his favorite cookies. Of her not yelling when he broke her favorite vase. Of her scrimping and saving so he could go to college. When the detective finally left the room once more the tears flowed freely. Perhaps even more so than Vicki, he was going to miss his sweet, wonderful mother.

Kim was surprised Larry was once more her patient. This time it was because he was under observation for any injuries he might have sustained from a jump to escape a fire. His mother had perished in that fire.

What was going on?

Any fool could see something was going on. This Taylor guy was in the middle of something big. Only question was: is he causing all these circumstances or was he a victim of them?

When Kim walked into Larry's room, his appearance was startling. Dark circles ringed his eyes and it looked as if he'd been doing a lot of crying. Even though he saw Kim, he said nothing.

"I'm sorry about your mother," Kim broke the silence.

"Tell that to your dear boyfriend who's involved in all this."

Kim was quiet. She was still rattled by seeing Josh Hillman at her apartment, even though Tony had given her a good reason why the man was there. "Let's not get into that," she said quietly.

"Look, you have to admit something's going on. Someone's out to get me and will apparently stop at nothing. I'm convinced Tony is in on it."

"OK. I'll agree something is going on. Maybe that for whatever reason somebody has it in for you. But you have to believe me Tony's not in on it."

"Then how did he come to cash in the MegaMoney ticket my wife was murdered for?"

Kim found herself becoming defensive. "He said he bought it and I believe him."

"Maybe there's a lot you don't know about this man. Perhaps he has a secret life you don't know about."

"Now you're being completely ridiculous," Kim said before leaving the room.

Yet she was fascinated with the Taylor case. She didn't think it would be possible that he would start a fire that would kill his own mother. Sure, he might have jumped into the harbor trying to take his own life, but this was different. There was something going on. She wanted to find out what that something was. Maybe then Taylor would leave Tony alone and Tony's name would be cleared from this mess. She would decide what to do later.

CHAPTER SEVENTEEN

The next day when Larry was released from County Hospital, he literally had no place to go. His mother's house no longer existed and he loathed to go back to the Newton home he and Vicki once shared. Still, that's where he had to go, at least to pack and get some money if he were to make that train to New York. He hopped into a cab that was in front of the hospital and gave the driver his Newton address.

It felt strange walking into the living room. It was the first time since Vicki's murder that he was in his own home. He felt anxious, totally freaked out. Vicki had been murdered in this very living room and the memory of seeing her body laid out on their white carpet was too much. He had to get what he came for and get out fast.

Larry went upstairs and began to pack items to take with him to New York. He just threw his clothes and toiletries haphazardly into an old gym bag. This place was giving him the creeps and who knew when his pursuer would strike again?

There. He was finished. Throwing the gym bag over his shoulder, Larry rushed downstairs. He was half way through the living room when the doorbell rang. Who was that? No one knew he was here. Scarcely able to breathe, Larry looked through a living room window. There on his doorstep stood Kimberly Long.

Larry didn't know what to do. Maybe Tony sent her here to lure him into a trap of some kind? Perhaps he was hiding nearby ready to kill him? Should he open the door and talk to her?

Curiosity won out and Larry opened the door.

"You left the hospital without saying good-bye," Kim scolded him.

"What are you doing here? How did you even know I was here?"

"With your mother's house burnt down, I figured you'd at least stop here. Listen, Mr. Taylor."

"You can call me Larry."

"OK, Larry. You've convinced me there is something going on. Even though I'm totally sure Tony has no part in all this, I do think someone is after you. That's where I can help."

"You help? How?"

"Well, Tony has this cabin up in New Hampshire. It's empty all the time. I think we've been up there only once since I've known him. I was thinking you could hide up there for a while, until the police figure out what's going on."

Fat chance. This had to be some kind of set-up. If he fell for it, he'd be walking into a death trap. Either Tony, or Hillman, or someone else would be waiting at this cabin to kill him. "Thanks for the offer, but no thanks."

"You should reconsider. Tony's place is the ideal place to hide away. It's secluded and no one would figure to look for you there. I'd be the only one who knew."

Yeah, right. "Actually, I've got some plans of my own. Thanks for coming by, but I really need to be going," he closed the door and started walking away.

"At least let me give you a ride."

"I don't think so," he briskly stared to walk in the direction of the Newton Highlands train stop, not bothering to look back. He paid the fare and descended the stairs to the train platform.

Twenty minutes passed and still no train to Boston. The platform was becoming crowded. Finally after forty minutes a train could be heard approaching the station. Everyone, including Larry, rushed to the edge of the platform to await the train.

Suddenly Larry felt two hands on his back and he was pushed forward. He lost his balance and fell into the train pit right in front of a speeding train.

Dazed, Larry tried to stand up. The train was so close now that he could actually feel the hot beam of its headlights. Inside, the conductor's face betrayed a mix of surprise and sheer horror.

Screeching, the train attempted to come to a stop. Larry squeezed his eyes shut out of terrifying fear. There was no place to jump out of the way, nowhere to hide. All he could think of to do was to lie down rigidly on the center of the track. Twice he had read of someone being saved of using this technique. Would he be the third?

With a deafening roar, followed by a magnificent gust of wind, the train thundered above him as it struggled to come to a halt. Larry lay still. Was he alive? Was he in one piece? He began to tremble, his every muscle jerking underneath his skin in a tremendous release of energy.

"Don't move. Help is on its way," someone shouted.

"I think I'm all right," Larry shouted back, moving each arm and leg to make sure it was still there.

Suddenly he became aware of a bright light. Was he having a near death experience? No, he was quite alive and someone was shining a bright flashlight in his direction.

"We'll have you out in a little while. There's an ambulance and fire truck on its way. Try not to move."

"I can move, so I think nothing's broken. I'm going to try to crawl to the front of the car so I can get out from these rows of wheels."

"Only if you think you can do it. If you're in any pain or discomfort, stay right where you are.

Inch by inch Larry crawled forward along the track. Above him the crowd waiting on the platform burst into applause as Larry head made it out from beneath the train.

One of the workers rushed to his side and pulled him completely out from underneath the vehicle.

"I think I can stand," Larry insisted, though he did feel a bit wobbly. With the man helping him, Larry was soon standing on his own two feet. This brought even more applause from the crowd.

Another transit worker rushed over and joined them. "There's a small ladder leading up to the platform a few feet away from here. With the two of us assisting you, do you think you can make it up to the platform?"

"I think so," Larry nodded. Soon he was sitting on a bench on the platform with the two train workers by his side.

"What happened?" one of them asked.

"I'm not sure," Larry mumbled. He was certain he had been pushed, but if he said anything and the police were called, they'd just write it off as another suicide attempt gone wrong. "When it became evident a train was approaching the station a lot of people surged forward and I must have stumbled. Stupid, huh?"

"Damn right. We're constantly advising riders to stand behind the yellow safety line. It's pure dumb luck that you weren't killed."

"Believe me, I know," Larry agreed.

"Here come the ambulance guys. They'll take you to the hospital to get checked out."

Two EMT's approached the bench. "You the guy who fell into the train pit?" one of them asked Larry.

"Yes."

"How are you feeling?"

"Considering what might have been, pretty damn lucky."

"You look shaken. How about a trip to the hospital so they can check you out?"

"No. I'm fine. Really." He had a train to New York City to catch in an hour.

"You really should let us take you," the other EMT said. "Sometimes there could be something seriously wrong with a person that doesn't become obvious until a lot later."

"Then I guess I'll take my chances because I'm not going to the hospital."

"You're sure now?" the EMT hesitated.

"Absolutely."

When the ambulance workers left, one of the transit workers turned to Larry. "We'd like some information from you so we can file it in our report. Then you're free to leave."

"What sort of information?"

The man took out a small notebook from his pocket along with a pen. "To begin with, we need your name and address."

There was no way Larry was going to give him that. "Martin. Martin Goodman. 116 Lakeside Drive."

"Boston?"

"Milton."

"Phone number?"

"Don't have one."

The transit worker gave Larry a funny look. "Martin, you say you just happened to stumble into the train pit?"

"That is correct."

"Is there anything else we should be made aware of?"

"Nope."

"I guess that's all we need to know for the time being."

"Actually, there is one more thing."

"What's that?"

"I had a large blue gym bag with me when I fell into the train pit. Can someone get it for me?"

"Is this it?" another subway worker approached the bench. One of our men brought it up a second ago."

"That's it," Larry took the bag. It was somewhat mangled from the whole ordeal but would last until he was able to get another one.

The subway workers indicated that they had to leave. "Will you still be taking the train to you destination, Mr. Goodman?"

"Yes," Larry nodded.

"Then may I suggest you stay good and far away from the edge of the platform," the man could not resist saying.

"I'll do that," Larry shouted at their retreating bodies. He meant it. He was not getting up off the bench he was seated on until the train was at a dead stop inside the station.

A few minutes later the train pulled in. Larry waited until it was at a complete stop and the doors were open before rushing inside. He managed to find a seat and slumped into it. What a day this was turning out to be! He never expected his would be killer would strike in the middle of the day with so many people around.

In a short while the subway train pulled into North Station and Larry got off. Walking briskly, he headed to Century Bank. He needed to withdraw all his money and close his account before he disappeared in the Big Apple.

After he closed his account, he would proceed to South Station to catch the Amtrak train to New York.

It wasn't too busy inside the band and it took only a few minutes to close his account. Now that he was five thousand dollars richer he suddenly felt nervous carrying all that money. He stuffed it into his gym bag and quickly left the bank. He headed down Winter Street, which would take him directly to South Station and the Amtrak terminal.

He didn't get very far when his mind screamed for him to stop.

There-coming out of Macy's Department Store! Wasn't that Tony Whiting? Larry had seen enough newspaper and news reports to memorize in detail what the man looked like.

His heart pounding wildly, he tapped the man on the back. "Excuse me, Mr. Whiting. Can I have a word with you?"

"Sure," Tony slowly turned around.

Wham! Larry's fist connected with Tony's nose, breaking it.

"What the . . ." Tony spattered as blood gushed from his nose and down his chin.

Larry punched him in the stomach, both fists slamming into the alleged lottery winner's body. He had to make Tony pay for being behind Vicki's death. Over and over Larry hit Tony as a crowd gathered to watch.

"Stop," Tony pleaded before falling to the ground.

Larry wasn't about to stop. He knew he should stop and leave, that a two o'clock train waited to take him to New York. However, he was possessed, and all he could do was to continue to beat Tony. Even if that meant killing the man.

In the end, it was the police who intervened and made Larry stop short of killing Tony. They pulled Larry off the man and slammed handcuffs on Larry's wrists. Then they forcefully threw Larry into a police wagon waiting nearby.

Why? Why did he have to veer from his plan of catching that Amtrak train and instead attack Tony Whiting? That's what Larry pondered as he lay on a smelly, old cot inside a police holding cell. What had his actions accomplished? Absolutely nothing. He hadn't even succeeded in killing Tony like he wanted to. Of all the rotten luck. Why couldn't the cops arrive two minutes later?

"Hey-you there-Taylor! I'm talking to you," a fat police sergeant wobbled up to Larry's cell. "We'll be moving you in five minutes."

"To where?"

"Oh, someplace you're very familiar with," the sergeant's lips curled up into something resembling a smile.

"Where might that be?" Larry wanted to know.

"You'll see," the sergeant turned around and was about to leave the area. "I need to ask you something," Larry remembered. "When I was arrested I had a bag with me. A blue, large size gym bag slightly mangled. I had it with me until I met up with Whiting. Has anyone found it?"

"No. No one said anything about a bag and it wasn't in any of the reports. Perhaps a pedestrian walked off with it."

"Probably that's what happened," Larry figured. Five thousand dollars. Gone. He could kiss New York City good-bye. Actually, he could kiss a lot of places good-bye since he had no more money.

"Ready to go?" a group of three officers approached the cell. "Let's move it."

One of the men used a key to open the cell and then handcuffed Larry.

"Where am I going?" Larry protested. He had a right to know where they were taking him.

The officers laughed amongst themselves.

"What's so funny," Larry demanded.

"You don't know where you're being taken?" came the answer. "Considering your past history and the way you beat up on Mr. Whiting, the judge thinks you're delusional. You've just been committed to spend another twenty-eight days at Harborside.

Luke was shaking badly as he picked up the phone. It had to be done. He had to once again explain to Mitchell why his latest attempt at eliminating Lawrence Taylor had failed. Probably Mitchell already knew. News of the fire was in both of the daily papers.

It was Mitchell's response that Luke feared. No doubt the man would yell, but all Luke wanted was another chance to prove himself. He wasn't even going to mention his botched attempt to kill Larry by pushing him into the subway pit right in the path of a speeding train.

Reluctantly, Luke dialed Mitchell's private number.

"Who's there?" Mitchell answered on the first ring.

"Rhino," Luke gave his new password.

"I've been waiting for you to call, Rhino," Mitchell spoke very, very slowly, as if speaking to a small child.

"I can explain," Luke began, dreading this conversation.

"I'm sure that you can."

"No, really I can," Luke agonized. "This Taylor guy. It's like he has nine lives. He must have escaped the fire from the sky window somehow. I had no way of knowing.

"You yourself know I've never screwed up a hit like this before. Basically, what I'm asking for is another chance. You know I'm good for it. What are the odds of something going wrong three times in a row?"

"No," Mitchell said firmly.

"What do you mean 'no'?" Luke coughed. He really needed the money this hit would provide.

"N-O. No Forget it. You're off the case. Have a nice life."

"Wait!" Luke cried helplessly as bubbles of cold sweat beaded up on his forehead.

"This isn't fair. What am I supposed to do?"

"Fry burgers at Mickey D's for all I care. We won't be needing your services any longer."

"Don't hang up," Luke pleaded. "I dig completely why you're so upset with me and I want to make amends. I'll do the hit at half off the regular rate just to make things right between us." It was a desperate offer, but he absolutely could not lose Mitchell as a customer.

"My, my, my. You're pathetic when you're desperate, you know that? Forget it. I've come up with a better idea to handle Taylor, one that doesn't involve murder.

Besides, the way you've handled this case has shaken my confidence in your abilities.

Your services will no longer be needed by this organization."

"But . . . but . . ." Luke stammered. "Let me prove myself to you. All I need is another chance. Please?"

"You already had another chance. How many chances do you need? The answer is no."

"Please don't cast me aside like this," Luke begged. "Think of all the help I've been to you throughout all these years."

"The key word is 'been'. It's obvious you've become careless and can no longer handle your duties. Go apply at Mickey D's. I understand they're hiring."

"Wait!" Luke shouted into the phone, but Mitchell had already hung up. Angrily, Luke smashed the mouthpiece of the pay phone against the ground, breaking it. A murderous rage solidified in his heart against Lawrence Taylor. Because of Taylor he was in this jam. How could that man have escaped so many attempts on his life?

Well, screw it. Luke wasn't going to listen to Mitchell. This time it was personal. He would track down and kill Mr. Taylor on his own time. If Mitchell paid him, fine. If not, that was OK, too. It didn't matter to him anymore. Larry had caused him to lose his best customer. That was reason enough for killing him.

CHAPTER EIGHTEEN

Larry was depressed to be back at Harborside. The only good thing about the situation was that even though he was on the same locked unit as before, he wasn't on the dreaded suicide watch. He could move around much more freely.

"Dr. Bellamy will see you now," Mel stuck his head into Larry's private room.

"Great," Larry got up. "I can hardly wait."

Dr. Bellamy was not in a good mood. "Have a seat. Detective Greene is in the day room and will be meeting with you right after our brief chat. Now, Mr. Taylor, I understand you severely beat up Tony Whiting earlier today. Can you tell me what happened."

"I wanted to kill the man for what he did to Vicki and my mother. He's involved in all this. When I ran into him at Downtown Crossing, it was like my emotions took over."

"That concerns me very much. The murder of your wife has damaged you in ways we cannot entirely predict. Mr. Whiting could have died because of you violently acting out these theories you have."

"It was bad luck I happened to run into him."

"Bad luck or not, you still weren't able to control your reaction. While you're under my care, we're going to have to work on that. I can see no other choice at this point but to put you on medication. You were hostile to that idea last time you were here, but now I see no other choice."

"Fine," Larry agreed. Anything to get out of here in four weeks. That's if he got out. He had visions of the hit man striking while he was a sitting duck on a locked unit.

"Well, it's good to hear you're at least being cooperative this time. Why don't I send Detective Greene in now? He really wants to speak with you."

"Do you know about what?"

"He didn't say. After he speaks with you, he'll be filling me in."

"Maybe he has some good news to report," Larry said hopefully. He skimmed through an old magazine while Dr. Bellamy went to get Detective Greene.

"Hello, Larry," Robert Greene closed the door behind him as he came in. He took a seat in the chair Dr. Bellamy had previously occupied. He reached into his pocket and took out a cigarette pack. "Dr. Bellamy gave me permission to smoke in here while I talk to you. Want one?" he asked Larry.

"Why not?" Larry agreed. He lit up and inhaled deeply.

Detective Greene did the same. He leaned back in his chair. "Tell me what's new, Lawrence?"

"I know what you're going to say. That I shouldn't have beat up on Whiting. Believe me, I know I shouldn't have."

"The man is in the hospital in guarded condition. But that's not actually why I'm here. How do you like being on the locked unit?"

"How do I like it? What kind of question is that? It sucks. I hate it."

"Well, you had better start getting used to the feeling."

"Why's that. As far as I'm concerned, I'm out of here in four weeks." Providing he himself was not murdered before then.

"You haven't been truthful with me Lawrence. The court doesn't take lightly to people who lie to police investigators."

"What on earth are you talking about? I've always been truthful with you. Stop talking in riddles."

"The only riddle here is how you'll react when I read your Miranda rights."

"Why? Am I being charged with something?"

The detective smiled and read Larry his rights.

"Tell me what's going on?"

"You're being charged with the murder of Mr. Rolando Torres. We found his body today in some woods off the Cape. We have eyewitnesses to you being the gunman. A Clark and Martina Cooper were working late in an office at 200 State Street. They saw you go in the building with Mr. Torres and saw you shoot the man outside later."

"They're lying!" Larry erupted. "If that's the case, why haven't they come forward sooner?"

"Fear. When they heard you were safely locked away on this locked unit, that's when they decided to come forward."

"I can't believe this," Larry nervously ran his fingers through his hair. "It doesn't even make sense. I kill Torres and then jump into the Boston Harbor? That's nuts!"

"That's exactly why you're here. Face it, Mr. Taylor. You're life is out of control and you're determined to bring down everyone else you can with you. Well, your little crime spree is over. In a matter of time, I hope to be able to tie you to the murder of your wife and mother also."

"You've got to listen to me. This Clark and Martina Cooper, whoever they are, are setting me up? It's obvious they're working with Whiting, Hillman, and whoever else is involved in this. Fifty million dollars is a lot of money."

Detective Greene yawned. "I'd be a rich man if I received a dime from every criminal who claims they're being set up. I need to be going. There'll be a court appointed lawyer in to see you sometime before you are transported from here to prison. Meantime, I hope you get the help you need."

The minute Greene left, Larry began shaking. The detective had not believed a single word Larry said. For a second Larry questioned his own sanity. What if he was imagining that whole conversation when Vicki told him she had hit the MegaMoney jackpot? What if there had been no phone call, as Josh Hillman claimed? What if he really was beginning to lose his mind and was responsible for all these crimes but did not know it? Was such a thing possible?

Mel burst into Bellamy's office, disturbing Larry's thoughts. "You have a visitor."

"Who is it?" Larry asked absently. No one cared about him anymore. Vicki was gone, his mother was gone.

"It's actually that girl who told you off in the smoking room last time you were here. You know, Whiting's girlfriend. Why is she here to see you?"

Larry couldn't understand it either.

"Should I send her away?" Mel asked.

"No, it's OK. I might as well see what she wants."

"There's an activities class going on in the day room, so I sent her to your room. Is that all right?"

"Fine," Larry said. He felt like a broken man of all life and energy as he walked to his room to see what Kimberly Long wanted.

"What the fuck were you thinking, beating up on Tony like that," Kim shrieked. "Do you know he came close to dying?"

"I'm sorry. The only reason I say that is because you're so upset. What I believe about Tony Whiting is only between Tony and me. I'm sorry if I hurt you in the process. I didn't purposefully track Tony down to attack him. I ran into him in town when I left you standing on my doorstep earlier and my emotions took over. You see, right after I left you, I headed to the Newton Highlands train station to catch a train to take me to downtown Boston. While I was waiting on the platform, I was pushed right into the train pit as a train was approaching."

"Yet you survived?" Kim was amazed.

"Barely. I feel it's only a matter of time before whoever is after me succeeds. And that's not all. This couple, these liars, are saying they saw me shoot a man by the name of Rolando Torres. Of course it isn't true, but the police seem to believe them. I'm being framed and am a sitting duck on this ward if whoever is after me wants to make a move."

"That's where I can help. I believe someone is out to get you and there's something going on. I told you about the cabin Tony has in New Hampshire we never go to. I think it'll be a good place for you to hide for the time being."

"What do you mean 'for the time being?' I'm on a locked ward, remember? After that, if I'm still alive, it's off to jail."

Kim looked at Larry slyly. "I have a plan."

Larry laughed. "What are you going to do? Bust me out of here?"

"Nothing that drastic. Tomorrow I'll come for you and get you out of here using my plan. You'll check into an area motel until I can drive you to New Hampshire. Trust me, the way you suspect Tony, no one will ever think of looking for you at his cabin."

Why was Kim so eager to get him to that cabin? Still, he had no alternative. Besides, he was starting to trust and like Kim.

Luke sat inside the Glass Slipper strip joint in Boston's Combat Zone nursing a beer. One of the strippers saddled up to him, rubbing her huge breasts against his arm. "What do you say, sugar?" she purred into his ear. "Buy me a drink?"

Ordinarily, Luke would be interested. But today he had something weighing on his mind. That something was Lawrence Taylor.

Damn that man! The son of a bitch was luckier than a cat with nine lives. By all standards, he should have been crushed underneath that train Luke had pushed him in front of earlier. Instead the man survives the incident with hardly a scratch. Angrily, Luke too a gulp of his beer. "I'm busy."

"You don't look busy to me," the stripper continued to rub her giant breasts against his arm. "How about it? One drink."

"Some other time," Luke said firmly.

"Suit yourself," the stripper went off to find a more interested man.

Think! Luke commanded his mind. He knew from the news that Taylor had been sent to Harborside following his attack on Whiting. Somehow he had to figure out a way of getting at him there.

An hour passed and Luke still didn't have a clue as to how to eliminate Taylor on the locked unit. Taylor was like a sitting duck cooped up on that unit if only Luke could figure out how to strike. Wearily he rubbed his eyes. All the smoking going on inside the club was making them watery. At that instant, he spotted someone he knew sitting across the room. What was the guy's name? Andrew? No, not Andrew. Angel? Yeah, that's it. Angel. Luke had bought some cocaine from the guy a while ago.

Suddenly, and idea began to formulate in Luke's mind. Why couldn't he somehow sneak on to the locked unit at night and inject Taylor with a massive overdose of cocaine? If anyone asked, he could say he was a new doctor or cleaning person or something.

Angel spotted Luke sitting across the room and gave him a half-hearted wave.

Come here, Luke motioned with his hand.

Lazily getting up from his seat, Angel picked up his drink and walked over to where Luke was sitting.

"I need to talk to you," Luke told Angel. "Not here. Can we go outside?"

"Sure," Angel agreed and followed Luke out of the club and into a deserted alleyway. "What's up? You looking to buy?"

"Possibly," Luke grinned. "See, I've got this problem. I need something so strong, so potent, that injected into a man would instantly kill him. Can you help me?"

"Sure, man. What you're looking for is a massive dose of fentanyl. I can get you that."

"When?"

"Tomorrow at three. I'll meet you at the Glass Slipper and give you a lethal dose of fentanyl in a syringe. Whatever you do with it is your business."

"Perfect. How much?"

"Five hundred dollars."

A bargain for getting rid of Taylor. "Deal," Luke smiled. Tomorrow night Taylor was going to be a dead man.

Why would someone be after Taylor? Kim couldn't help wondering. Could Tony really have somehow gotten his hands on a lottery ticket Taylor's wife was murdered for?

It just didn't make any sense. She trusted Tony. There had to be another angle. If only she could figure out what it was. She thought of a patient that was once on her unit. A lovely black woman called Ettie Williams. Ettie was a private investigator and they had hit it off. In fact, Ettie insisted that Kim call her sometime. Kim decided this would be a good time to do so. She looked up Ettie's number in her address book and dialed it.

"Hello," a pleasant voice picked up.

"Hi Ettie. It's Kim Long. Remember me."

"Of course. You're the wonderful woman who was my nurse when I was a patient at County Hospital. I'm so glad you called. How are you dear?"

"Not so good. I'm sure you've read about a Lawrence Taylor accusing Tony Whiting of having something to do with the murder of Larry's wife. Mr. Taylor alleges his wife was in possession of a winning MegaMoney ticket before she was killed and that this is the ticket Tony cashed in. Well, Tony is my boyfriend and I don't think he'd hurt a fly. He has plenty of money and doesn't need to murder someone to get more. That said, I think something is going on. Mr. Taylor was a patient of mine after two strange incidents recently. I'm trying to help him because I believe someone is out to get him. In one incident he barely escaped a fire. His mother died in that fire. In another he was plucked out of Boston harbor after jumping in to escape someone he claims was shooting at him. A man named Rolando Torres was murdered that same night and now these people have come forward saying they saw Larry shoot Mr. Torres, which of course Larry denies. But the thing is, I become convinced someone is after Mr. Taylor. The police are ready to close this case and lock Larry away at least for the murder of Mr. Torres and just now I thought of you and remembered you did some private investigating. Can you somehow look into these people accusing Mr. Taylor? I don't know their names, but I can find out for you."

"That's quite an assignment," Ettie laughed. "I wish I could help you, but first off, I only investigate missing persons. This is way out of my league. Have you considered this Taylor guy might be lying about his wife ever having a winning MegaMoney ticket? He could have murdered her himself and just be throwing suspicion on your boyfriend Tony. That's personally what I think. I'd be very, very careful of getting involved helping Larry. Now that's only my advice, but I like you Kim and I don't want to see you get hurt because this Lawrence Taylor is a criminal. I'm glad you called me. However, I can't help you."

"That's OK," Kim disappointingly hung up the phone.

CHAPTER NINETEEN

K im made two stops before arriving at Harborside the next day. One stop was at Bloomingdale's and the other one was at Wig World. She stuffed her purchases into her ample shoulder bag and and arrived at Harborside at two-thirty in the afternoon. Good. The nurses changed shifts at three. She was let on the unit with no problem and went straight to Larry's room. There she found him sleeping. "Hey-sleepyhead. Wake up," she nudged him.

"Whoa . . ." Larry's eyes flew open and he sat up before noticing who it was. "Oh, it's only you," he said with relief.

"Only me," Kim pretended to be insulted. "I'm the woman who's going to get you out of here."

"I was up half the night because every noise I heard, I was convinced it was my would-be killer coming to get me. Finally, I was so tired I couldn't help falling asleep."

"Understood," Kim patted her large shoulder bag. "In here is everything I need to get you out of this joint."

"What are you talking about? All the nurses, doctors and mental health workers here know what I look like. They're not about to open the door for me so I can just waltz out of here."

"Maybe for you they won't, but for me and my girlfriend who came here to visit you they will."

"Girlfriend?" Larry slowly began to get the idea. "Oh, no. Wait a minute. It'll never work."

"Why not? Half the battle is won. They never asked to check the contents of my handbag. A wig. A little make-up. Top it all off with a baggy, long raincoat you'll put on and it might work."

Larry glanced out the window. "It's not even raining out," he observed.

"Who cares? It's cloudy out, isn't it? Now go into the bathroom and transform yourself. The nurses will be changing shift in fifteen minutes. Those that just come on won't know I came here alone. They'll open the door to let me and my friend off the unit."

"I'm telling you, you're nuts. This isn't going to work."

"Do you have any better ideas? Do you?"

"No, but this is insanity."

"Here," Kim handed Larry her bag. "I want you to march into that rest room and start doing yourself up. Don' t come out until you're ready. I'll knock on the door to let you know the coast is clear."

"I can't believe I'm doing this," Larry said, taking the bag and entering the small bathroom connected to his hospital room. Once inside he looked into the mirror. Could he do it? Could he really pass as a woman?

He started by washing his face. Next he opened the Kim's bag. He'd never put on make-up before, but he had seen his wife Vicki do so countless times when she was alive.

The beige stuff in the glass bottle was the foundation, so he put that on first, massaging it into his skin. Next came the concealer, which he dabbed under his eyes and around his lips. He applied the blush in swift motions away from the face as Vicki used to do. The mascara and eyeshadow took a little patience but he didn't bungle the job too badly. Finally he was ready for the lipstick and wondered what color Kim had stuck him with. Red. He never thought he'd see the day come where he'd be forced to put on red lipstick.

Now he was ready for the wig. Gingerly he removed it from the box, not sure how to put it on. There was a tag sown inside on one end, so that must be the back. He put it on and stepped back from the mirror. So this is what he looked like as a blonde female. Taking a comb from the bad, he combed the wig's hair until it was full and fluffy. Could he really fool anyone on the nursing staff into letting him off the unit?

He held off on any judgment until he put the black, long raincoat on. It was big and baggy and hid his masculine frame well. Maybe, just maybe, this crazy scheme might just work.

A knock on the door interrupted his thoughts. "Are you almost done?"

"Just about."

Kim entered the bathroom and closed the door after her. "Let me see," she looked him over. "This is going to work."

"What if it doesn't? Then the police will really think I'm guilty because I was trying to escape. That's more jail time."

"Provided the guy after you doesn't get to you first," Kim reminded him. "That's why you have to get the hell out of here."

"I know," Larry nervously ran his hand through the wig's blonde hair. "It's just that I'm scared this isn't going to work."

"So am I, but we need to try. You really look like a woman. I think we can pull this off."

"I hope so," Larry tried to calm himself down.

"We'll walk down the corridor together towards the nurses station. I'll say we need to be let out. If whoever's on isn't paying too much attention, we should be let off in a flash. Try not to act too nervous."

"I'll try," Larry said nervously.

"Ready?"

"I guess."

"Good. Let's do it."

They were about to leave the room when Larry pulled back.

"What's wrong?" Kim whispered.

"That black man standing near the day room. His name is Mel and he's a pretty sharp cookie. I don't think we can fool him."

"What do you suggest we do?"

"Wait until he goes inside the day room or gets called away."

"OK. But we can't chance remaining in this room too long either. Someone's bound to figure out they haven't seen you in a while and come looking for you."

"Give it a few minutes," Larry said. Sure enough, Dr. Bellamy soon appeared and summoned Mel into his office.

"Let's go," Kim said. Together she and Larry approached the nurse's station. There was only one nurse sitting there going through some charts. "Can I help you?" she asked.

"Yes," Kim stated. "We need to be let off the unit."

"Whom were you visiting?"

"Lawrence Taylor," Kim said anxiously. Would they be able to pull it off?

"Follow me," the nurse went around the circular desk and walked them to the door.

Larry held his breath as she inserted the key and slowly turned it.

"You know, you look very familiar," she turned to Larry.

Larry began to panic. He dare no say anything in his masculine voice.

Kim came to the rescue. "This is a distant cousin of Mr. Taylor."

"That's probably what it is," the young nurse reasoned. "I can see the resemblance." She turned the key all the way and Larry and Kim walked off the unit.

"Your plan really worked," Larry said in amazement.

"Shhh. Let's get out of the hospital first."

Soon they were seated in Kim's blue BMW. Impulsively, Larry reached over and gave her a hug. "We did it!"

Kim hugged him back with feeling.

"Where are we going?" Larry wondered.

"I can't drive you to Tony's cabin in New Hampshire tonight or have you stay at the Towers because security would wonder who you were. I know of this small motel in Canton. Actually calling it a motel is being rather generous. A lot of characters and low lifes live there, but it's out of Boston and no one would think of looking for you there. The management couldn't care less what goes on. You'll stay there for the night. Tomorrow in the morning I'll come for you and drive you to New Hampshire."

"I really appreciate all you're doing for me," Larry said gratefully as they pulled out of the Harborside parking lot. "Especially because of what I did to Tony. If it weren't for you doing this, I believe my would-be hitman would have somehow gotten to me and killed me on the locked unit."

"Could be," Kim agreed. They drove in silence until Kim pulled into a shopping mall.

"Why are we stopping here?" Larry asked.

"To buy stuff such as clothes and food you'll need in New Hampshire. It'll be a while before I'm able to drive up and bring more."

"You think of everything," Larry said.

"We'll need to be quick about it. Probably by now Harborside has figured out you're not there and alerted the police. We have to make this a very fast shopping spree."

"Lead the way," Larry agreed.

Luke arrived at the Glass Slipper strip club exactly at three. Immediately the big-breasted stripper from yesterday came right over to him. "Care to buy me a drink today?" she sat down next to him.

"Sure, why not?" Luke decided. Within hours he would be emptying a syringeful of fentanyl into Larry Taylor and getting his revenge. That was reason enough to put him in a good mood.

The dancer ordered her drink and sipped it through a straw. "My name's Judy. What's yours?"

"Luke."

"It's a pleasure to be joining you, Luke. I just started working here. Would you care to join me at my place after my shift is over?"

"Can't tonight," Luke explained. "I'm waiting for someone and then I have something to do. Perhaps another time?"

"I'd like that," Judy smiled at Luke.

Suddenly Luke spotted Angel entering the club. "Excuse me," he got up. "I'll see you some other time," he told Judy and went to join Angel. They walked outside and into the alleyway near the club.

"Do you have it?" Luke asked eagerly.

"Sure do," Angel grinned. "Do you have the money?"

"Right here," Luke handed him a wad of bills.

Angel took a moment to count them. "Yep, all here. They syringe is in a paper bag in my car. Wait here for me and I'll be right back with it."

Anxiously Luke hung around the alley waiting for Angel to return. It seemed he had been gone an awful long time. Luke was beginning to worry. What if Angel had just pulled a fast one on him and taken off with his money? But his worrying was for nothing as Angel soon appeared with a paper bag in his hand. "Be very, very careful with the syringe," Angel explained. "Don't take it out of the bag until you're ready to use it so you don't accidentally prick yourself with it. There's a lethal dose in there, just like you asked for."

"Thanks, man," Luke gingerly took the small paper bag from Angel.

"Let me know if you need anything else," Angel started to walk away. "I can get just about anything."

"I will," Luke called after him. He hopped into his beat up car and drove up to Harborside with the intention of seeing just how easy it would be to get on the locked unit. But something was very wrong. He could tell that the minute he drove into the parking lot. The place was full of not only police, but police with dogs. They seemed to be searching the grounds of Harborside and beyond. He locked the paper bag containing the syringe in the glove compartment of his car and hopped out.

Inside the hospital's main lobby he obtained directions to the locked unit. Calm down, he told himself as he proceeded towards it. All the cops and dogs outside couldn't possibly have anything to do with Lawrence Taylor.

He paused before the heavy door of the locked unit and pressed the buzzer. A young, overweight nurse came over and opened the door.

"I'm here to visit Mr. Lawrence Taylor," he said directly.

"That's not possible," the nurse shrugged. She looked distraught and Luke wondered if she had been crying.

"Why not?" Luke wondered.

"Because he escaped this afternoon."

"What do you mean he escaped this afternoon!" Luke blew up. He had no idea where to look for Taylor now. "What kind of mickey-mouse security do you people have."

"It was actually my fault," the nurse admitted. "I didn't know it was Mr. Taylor when I let him leave. He was disguised as a woman and before I realized what I have done he was already let out."

Luke felt sick to his stomach. "He was disguised as a woman?"

"Yes. He had on a blonde wig and a black raincoat. A woman with black hair wearing a green dress was with him. But why am I telling you all this? I've already told the police everything I could remember and now my job may be in jeopardy. You're not with the police, are you?"

"No, I'm just a friend of Mr. Taylor's. You wouldn't have any idea where Mr. Taylor might go, would you?"

"No idea. I've got to get back to work," the nurse slammed the door in Luke's face.

DAMN! Luke was angry and not sure what to do next. He climbed into his car and drove to his motel and parked near the pay phones. Somehow he had to set things right with Mitchell. That was his only hope of ever working in Boston again.

Nervously he got out of the car and put some change into the phone. He dialed Mitchell's private number but there was no answer. He was about to try again when a red Mercedes pulled into the parking lot and drove up to the registration cabin of the motel. A girl with long black hair wearing a green dress hopped out of the vehicle and ran inside the registration cabin. Luke's heart began to beat faster. Didn't that young nurse over at Harborside say the woman who helped Taylor get off the unit was wearing a green dress and had long black hair? He had to get a look at who was seated at the passenger's side of the car.

The sun was in his eyes, so he took a few steps and pretended to use another of the pay phones, which was in the shade. Whoever was sitting in the passenger's side had curly blonde hair and was wearing a black coat! This fleabag motel must be where Taylor planned on hiding out.

Luke watched as the girl came out of the registration cabin and got into the BMW. They pulled into the parking space in front of cabin number 17. After about a minute, Taylor, still in disguise got out of the car and let himself into cabin 17. Then the girl in the car sped away.

What luck. This was Luke's lucky day after all. Only fate would deliver Taylor like this to him after all. That night, when he was reasonably certain Larry might be asleep, Luke would break into cabin 17 and inject the fentanyl into Taylor's soon to be lifeless body. Mr. Taylor was not going to be the hit that got away and he, Luke, would retain his one hundred accuracy rate of hunting down his target. It made him tremble with glee. He couldn't wait for nighttime to arrive.

Once inside the cabin Larry locked and bolted the cheap door, wondering if it would help any. If someone really wanted to they'd be able to break-in without a problem anyways. But no one knew he was here and that put his mind at ease.

Tired, he lay down on the lumpy bed in the center of the room. It was highly unbelievable the way he was able to just walk off the locked unit at Harborside. To relieve some of the tension, he couldn't help laughing. Imagine, someone like him putting on a blonde wig, a little make-up, and actually passing as a woman. But he had done it, and here he was, waiting for Kim to take him to some deserted cabin in New Hampshire tomorrow morning.

He removed his wig and placed it on the nightstand beside the bed. It had been making his scalp itch and he scratched it using both hands. That made him fell better. An exhausted yawn escaped his lips and he curled up on the uncomfortable bed for a nap.

What a long nap it turned out to be. He didn't awaken until almost midnight, still feeling groggy-eyed. Struggling into the bathroom, he dared to look into the mirror. He looked like shit. The mascara he had on was smudged all over his face and the same went for the lipstick. What he needed was a nice, hot shower to invigorate him and remove all the make-up. Larry couldn't wait to start feeling like a man again.

Taking off all his clothes, he eagerly turned the shower knob, waiting for the hot water. "What is this?" he muttered to himself. Why the hell wasn't there any water coming from the shower head? For a minute he stood there, as if staring at the shower nozzle would somehow make the water come out. "Damn," he realized mental telepathy wasn't going to work. Removing what make-up he could, Larry put on a sweatshirt and jeans he and Kim had bought earlier and walked into the bedroom to call management.

"What is it?" a sleepy sounding voice at the registration desk picked up on the eighth ring.

"This is Adam Slate," Larry gave the name he was checked in under. "I'm having a problem in suite 17. I seems the shower isn't working."

"That's impossible," the man yawned.

Larry found himself becoming angry. "What do you mean that's impossible? I just tried to take a shower and not even a drop of water came out. How long before you can send someone to fix it?"

"I'll make a note of it. Someone should be there to take a look at it tomorrow afternoon."

"I'm not going to be here tomorrow afternoon and I want take a shower right now," Larry made clear.

"Look, mister. Get a grip. There's nothing I can do this time of night, unless . . ."

"Unless what?"

"Unless you want to change rooms. All our cabins are filled up for tonight except for number 47. If you want to come by and get a key for it, I'll be glad to switch you."

"I'll be there in ten minutes," Larry quickly hung up. Then he started having second thoughts. What if the guy at the registration desk recognized him as the escaped mental patient? Nah, as Kim said, in this sleazy place even if the guy did it wouldn't matter to him.

Quickly Larry went to the registration cabin and got the key to cabin 47. He was glad he had switched. Even upon entering, cabin 47 didn't have the old, musty odor that cabin 17 had. It seemed cleaner too. Larry locked and bolted the flimsy door and went into the bathroom. After relieving himself, he turned on the shower. Warm, wonderful water gushed out from the overhead nozzle. He threw off his clothes and jumped in.

Twenty minutes later he emerged, drying himself with one of the small, scratchy towels the motel provided. He sat down on the edge of the bed and dialed the number Kim had given him before she drove off.

"Hello," her sleepy voice answered.

"Sorry to bother you," Larry told her.

"Is there a problem?"

"I'm fine," he reassured her. "I'm sorry for waking you but I needed to let you know I've changed rooms. I'm now in cabin 47."

"Why'd you do that for?"

"Because the shower wasn't working in cabin 17."

"You shouldn't have done that. I watched the late news and there was a report on how you escaped from Harborside following being charged with the murder of Rolando Torres. What if the guy at the registration desk recognized you? I don't think he'd call the cops, but you can't be too careful."

"I thought of that but I really wanted to take a hot shower."

"What am I going to do with you?" Kim groaned. "Whatever you do, just stay put where you are. Don't even think of venturing outside. I'll be there tomorrow morning like I said I would."

"I'll see you then. Sorry for waking you," Larry apologized.

"I guess I can forgive you this one time," Kim joked. "Good-night."

"Good-night," Larry said, aware of how much he was beginning to like Kim.

Desmond Goodson felt tired. He had been driving his truck ten hours straight and needed to get some rest. The first hotel or motel he came across, he would stop for the night.

Several minutes later he saw a billboard advertising the Chelsea Motel at the next exit. He took that exit and a few minutes later pulled up to the registration cabin of the Chelsea Motel. The place looked dumpy, exactly the sort of place a murderer might want to hide out, he shivered. But Desmond was tired and hopped out of his truck. He certainly didn't need a palace to stay in. As long as the place had a bed and a pillow, he would be happy.

The man at the registration desk was sleeping. "Excuse me," Desmond shook him lightly. "I'm looking for a room."

"Room?" The man was confused for a second. "I'm afraid we don't have any rooms left. We're full tonight."

"Thanks," Desmond turned to leave. As tired as he was, perhaps it was just as well. The place was dumpier than he thought. When he was talking to the man he had noticed a mouse scurry by the back of the desk.

"Wait," the man at the desk called after Desmond as if he had just remembered something. "I might be able to help you after all."

"How's that?" Desmond paused.

"Actually, I do have one room that's available. There's something wrong with it, though. The fellow that was in it before dropped by the key a short while ago."

"What's wrong with it?" Desmond dared to ask.

"The shower ain't working."

"That's all?"

"That's it."

Desmond thought it over for a minute and decided he could live without taking a shower for one night. Besides, he was too damned tired to be driving around anymore. "I'll take it," he said. "How much?"

"I'll let you have it for fifty bucks seeing the shower ain't working."

"I'll give you thirty."

"Make it forty and you've got yourself a room."

Desmond peeled four ten-dollar bills from his wallet and slid them across the counter to the man. Surprisingly, he wasn't asked to provide identification of any kind.

"Is that it?" he asked.

"Make sure you're out of the room by noon if you ain't staying any additional nights."

"Oh, I'll be out way before then," Desmond promised. He wanted to get back on the road at nine or earlier. He took the key from the man.

"Your cabin is number 17. Good-night."

"Good-night," Desmond left the registration cabin and let himself into cabin 17. The room was dirty and smelled funny, but at least it had a bed. Desmond went into the bathroom and turned on the shower just to make sure it wasn't working. It wasn't. The old pipes creaked and groaned but not a single drop of water came out. He took all his clothes off except his underwear and climbed into bed. Reaching over, he shut off the bedside lamp and instantaneously fell into a deep, much needed, sleep.

At three a.m. his alarm clock went off, just as Luke had set it to. Joyfully, Luke crawled out of bed and put on some dark clothes. Quietly, very quietly, he left his cabin and went to his car. He removed a crowbar from the trunk and then the paper bag with the syringe from the glove compartment. His heart was beating wildly as he looked over the area to make sure no one would see him. None of the motel cabins had lights on and the parking lot was deserted. Crowbar in one hand, paper bag in the other, Luke crept towards cabin 17. He put the paper bag down and swiftly shoved the crowbar into the cheap wooden door and applied pressure. Luke was surprised at how easily the flimsy lock and bolt gave. He picked up the paper bag and walked into the dark cabin.

He could make out the form of Taylor asleep on the bed. The man was snoring like an ox. Evidently Taylor was a sound sleeper.

Trying not to make too much noise, Luke took out the syringe from the paper bag. His hands were shaking badly. He had never handled a lethal dose of a narcotic before.

Deciding he needed to act quickly, Luke pulled the blanket off the bed. Taylor was sleeping on his stomach, his head away from Luke. Also, he was naked except for a pair of white underwear, which was good. Still asleep, Taylor groaned. DO IT NOW! Luke's mind screamed. With his left hand Luke pulled down the man's underwear while his right hand shoved the syringe deep into Taylor's right buttock. The needle went in with hardly any resistance. Trembling, Luke depressed the plunger and emptied the syringeful of fentanyl.

"What the . . ." Taylor tried to sit up.

Reacting impulsively, Luke grabbed the heavy lamp on the night table and bashed Taylor on the head with it. That seemed to do the trick. Like a wet noodle, Taylor flopped back on the bed. It was over. Ha-ha, Luke couldn't resist a laugh. He had won. In the end, Taylor just couldn't outsmart Boston's number one hitman. Luke felt very victorious. He just had to see the fruits of his labor. He took the lamp he had just bashed Taylor in the head with and turned it on. All of a sudden Luke felt sick to his stomach. The man he had just killed was not Lawrence Taylor.

CHAPTER TWENTY

Larry spent an uneventful morning inside cabin 47 as he waited for Kim to arrive. He was getting hungry but dared not leave the room in case anyone recognized him. Besides, any minute now Kim might arrive.

Finally the anticipated knock on the front door came. "Larry-it's me, Kim. Open up."

Larry slid open the bolt and let Kim inside.

"How was your night?" she asked. "Was the shower functioning satisfactorily in this cabin?"

"As a matter of fact, it was. I even got to take another one this morning while I waited for you."

"Good. Are you ready to go?"

"I am. What do you want me to do with the blonde wig and make-up?"

"We'll dump them in the dumpster outside."

"I don't know how you women do it. The wig made my scalp all itchy and the make-up irritated my skin. It still doesn't feel quite right."

"Poor baby," Kim laughed. "Let's get going. Tony is getting released from the hospital today and I want to be back as soon as possible. Are you hungry?"

"Starved."

"There's a drive through McDonald's on the way. Can you deal with MickeyD's?"

"I'm so hungry, I could eat just about anything."

After a quick meal of burgers and french fries, they were speeding in Kim's BMW towards New Hampshire. "I packed a little something extra for you," Kim told Larry. "There's a shot gun in the back seat for you to have in case you encounter any wild animal or something. Let's hope you never have to use it."

"I hope not." Despite what Detective Greene might think, Larry had never before handled a gun.

"Did I tell you there's no phone service at the cabin? The area's too secluded. There won't be a way for you to reach me or anyone else. The food we bough yesterday should last at least a month. I'll be back with more way before then."

"So this is what my life's become. Hiding out in seclusion waiting for my next food delivery."

"Beats being in jail or dead," Kim reasoned.

Larry had his doubts so he didn't respond. Instead he looked out the window and with each mile watched the woods become thicker and more pristine. It was a long time since he had been this far away from the city. "So tell me," he finally asked Kim. "How did you happen to meet Tony?"

"We met at an art gallery when I was in nursing school. He's a lot older than I am, you know. But we found personality wise we had a lot in common. I'm certain he had nothing to do with the murder of your wife," Kim added.

"Do you love him?"

"Yes, in many ways."

"But you're not sure."

"I'm as sure as I can be at this time. What about you? How did you meet Vicki?"

"At a meditation class. I asked her out and soon after we were married."

"Any kids?"

"None. What about you and Tony?"

"We don't have any either, but I imagine if we're together in the future we will start a family."

"I really appreciate you helping me like this. I never thought Whiting's girlfriend, of all people, would go out of her way to help me."

"That's because I believe someone really is out to get you. I don't believe you could have killed your own mother or wife like that. Or Mr. Torres."

"I didn't. But now the police have these two so called witnesses accusing me of killing Torres and they're ready to close the book on all this. I can't believe the mess my life has become."

"Try to relax," Kim urged. "I'll wake you up when we get to the cabin."

Luke groaned. It was Friday afternoon and he did not want to get up. Why couldn't he just fall asleep forever? He couldn't remember a time when he felt more depressed. How he wished Mitchell had never chosen him to eliminate Taylor. Just the mention of the man's name made Luke sick to his stomach.

The first thing Luke did after getting dressed was to walk over to the pay phones outside the Chelsea Motel and try to call Mitchell. There was no answer. Standing there, deciding what to do next, Luke couldn't resist glancing over at cabin 17. It was only a matter of time before the body in it was discovered. Poor man. At least Mitchell would never know how badly he had bungled this latest attempt. Despite all his flops, Luke still entertained the idea of Mitchell taking him back into the organization someday.

Luke decided to drive down to Boston's Combat Zone. He went into the Glass Slipper. Judy was on stage and she waved to Luke when he walked in. Not feeling sociable, Luke walked out and went into a bar called Harry's. There no one should bother him while he got good and drunk.

Hours later, he was completely drunk when he noticed Ettie Williams come into the bar. He knew she was a private investigator of some sort, but walked over to her and sat down. Many times in the past they had talked and Luke had a liking for her.

"Hi, Luke," Ettie smiled. "How are you?"

"Drunk," Luke burped.

"I can see that," Ettie laughed. "I just stopped by for a quick drink. What are you drinking? I'll buy you one."

"A rum and coke."

"Two rum and cokes," Ettie told the bartender.

"Thank you," Luke slurred. "I'm mighty low on money."

"You need to hit the lottery," Ettie smiled.

"Fat chance," Luke said angrily.

Ettie noticed Luke's change of mood. "What do you mean? You have the same chance of doing so as the rest of us."

"Boy, are you naïve. The damn lottery is fixed."

"I don't believe you."

"Mark my words. Tomorrow night's MegaMoney winner is going to be Richard Strock." He had seen a list of up-coming winners the last time he was at Mitchell's.

"And how do you happen to know all this," Ettie played along with him.

"I work . . . I mean, I used to work, for this guy called Mitchell. He ordered the hit on that Taylor woman. She really did have a winning MegaMoney ticket, you know."

"That's amazing," Ettie sipped her rum and coke, not sure whether to believe what Luke in his drunk state was telling her. "So how did Tony Whiting get to cash in the ticket."

Suddenly Luke realized he had said too much. Way, way, too much. "I gotta go," he slurred, and as quickly as he could left the bar.

It was early afternoon when Kim and Larry arrived at the cabin. They quickly brought in the bags of food and put them in the pantry. Larry put the shotgun in the kitchen area, praying he'd never have to use it. They cleaned the log cabin up a little bit and soon Kim had to leave. Impulsively, Larry gave her a kiss. "You know, I wish we could have met under different circumstances."

"So don't I," Kim found herself agreeing. But she had to head back to Boston to be with Tony when he got out of the hospital. "I'll be here in around a month to check on you and bring you more food. Then we'll decide what to do."

"I can't wait," Larry said.

Luke Spiros was getting a terrible headache as he walked the streets of Boston's Combat Zone. He couldn't believe all the information he had told Ettie about Mitchell and who tonight's winning MegaMoney winner would be. What could he have possibly been thinking? Now he had to get rid of Ettie before tonight's big drawing.

He went back to Harry's bar but Ettie was no longer there. However, Luke knew where her small Chinatown office was and as quickly as his drunken state would allow, started walking towards it.

Tony Whiting let himself into his penthouse apartment, thinking Kim would be there to greet him. "Kim-I'm home," he called. Where was she? She had told him she would be there for him when he was released from the hospital.

Still feeling badly bruised from the beating Taylor had given him, Tony made a cup of hot tea and sat down in his favorite recliner in the living room. It was good to be home.

Suddenly the phone rang and Tony answered it, hoping it might be Kim. "Hello."

"Is Kim there?" a pleasant voice asked.

"No, she isn't."

"Will she be in soon?"

"I'm not sure. I presume so."

"This is Ettie Williams. It's really important. Can you have her give me a call the second she gets in?"

"I'll make sure she gets the message," Tony promised, hanging up the phone and sinking back into the chair. Who the hell was Ettie Williams, he wondered.

He didn't get a chance to relax for very long as once again the phone rang. This time it was Kim.

"Kim!" Tony exclaimed, happy to hear from her. "Where are you? You were supposed to be here when I got home."

"Something came up but I'm on my way home now. I'll be there as soon as I can. How are you?"

"Sore. Sore all over. But the sight of you will make me feel much better. Hurry."

"I will," Kim promised, about to hang up.

"Wait!" Tony remembered about the phone call. "Some woman called Ettie Williams called here for you. She said it's really important she talk with you."

"Thanks. I'll give her a call right now."

Ettie sat in her small office waiting for Kim to call. Perhaps she was over-reacting, but she wanted to tell Kim what Luke had told her. She was curious herself. Would Richard Strock win the MegaMoney drawing tonight?

When the phone rang, Ettie picked it up on the first ring.

"Hello, Ettie?"

"Kim, I'm so glad you called me."

"What's up?"

"Probably nothing, but I just had an interesting conversation with someone known as Luke Spiros. Anyways, he was really drunk, but said a couple of interesting thing. For one, he claimed someone named Mitchell ordered the hit on Victoria Taylor for her winning MegaMoney ticket."

"No," Kim gasped.

"As I said, the guy was very drunk. But there is a way to know if he was telling the truth. According to Luke, the MegaMoney game is somehow fixed in advance and someone called Richard Strock is supposed to win tonight."

At that moment, the door to Ettie's small office flew open and an enraged Luke strode in.

"Luke—what are you doing here?" a startled Ettie asked.

Calmly Luke his gun out of his shoulder holster and fired.

Kim heard the noise. "Ettie, are you all right?" she screamed. There was no answer.

Trembling, Kim called 911 and told them to send an ambulance to Ettie's address. Was this guy Luke right that the MegaMoney game was fixed? She had to tell someone Richard Strock would be tonight's winner before he actually became so. Since she passed Lottery Headquarters in Hingham on her drive to Boston, she would stop there.

Lottery headquarters was a massive building occupying many acres in Braintree. Signs were clearly posted directing visitors to the main entrance, so Kim had no problem finding it. Inside there was an information desk and Kim ran up to the woman behind it.

"Can I speak with the director of the lottery?" Kim inquired, not sure who to ask for but deciding to start at the top.

"He's a very busy man. What's this regarding?"

"Tonight's lottery drawing. I have reason to believe it might be fixed."

The woman yawned. "Honey, ain't no way the lottery could be fixed. They system's foolproof. Besides, the director just left," the woman pointed to a man exiting from one of the side doors. "So I guess you're out of luck. I wouldn't lose any sleep over it. Like I said, there isn't any way the lottery could be f . . ."

Kim wasn't listening. Flying down the steps of the front entrance she raced around to the side of the building where the exit was the director had just left from.

"Wait!" she shouted to the man as he was about to climb into an expensive car.

The man paused, waiting to see what she wanted. "Can I help you, young lady?"

"Are you the director of the state lottery?"

"I am."

"So you're in charge of the MegaMoney drawings."

"That's correct. My name's Charles Modine. What can I do for you?"

"Mr. Modine, I know this is going to sound crazy, but I have reason to believe tonight's and other nights MegaMoney drawings might be fixed."

Modine smiled. "Let me assure you, young lady, that such a thing is not possible. Where did you get a crazy idea like that?"

"A woman I know called Ettie Williams was told so by a Luke Spiros. He told her that the Taylor woman was killed for a ticket and tonight's winner would be Richard Strock. When I was on the phone with her, this Luke guy I think shot her. There's got to be something going on."

"The names mean nothing to me," Modine said thoughtfully. "I'm sorry you think your friend was hurt, but the Spiros guy had to be joking. Nothing can get past our security system we have in place for MegaMoney."

"What if someone called Richard Strock won tonight. Then would you believe Luke was right."

"If Mr. Richard Strock does win tonight, I can assure you I'd launch the most aggressive investigation the lottery ever did see. But there's no way he's going to hit. Like I said, our security system is second to none."

"Still, you'll investigate if Richard Strock claims the MegaMoney drawing?"

"I give you my word."

"In that case, I'm glad I caught up with you to tell you all this. I wasn't sure who I should be speaking with."

"You came to the right person. Anything happening with the lottery is my business."

"I just hope my friend Ettie is all right and that they catch Luke Spiros."

"So do I," Modine nodded. "Now, if you'll excuse me, I'm running late for a meeting. It was nice meeting you, Ms . . . ?"

"Long. Thank you for hearing me out."

"Anytime."

Kim shook Modine's hand and then he drove away. She felt relieved at telling him everything Ettie had told her. If there was anything going on with the MegaMoney game, she felt confident Modine would look into it. She was about to hop into her car and drive away when she spotted a pay phone by the side of the lottery building. She walked over to it to call Tony. So much had happened since she last spoke with him that she decided to tell him everything.

"Kim," Tony picked up the phone. "I was expecting you home by now."

"I am on my way this time, I promise. So much has happened."

"What are you talking about?"

Kim took a deep breath. "I helped Larry Taylor escape from Harborside yesterday."

"What!" Tony screamed. "Are you nuts? You can get in serious trouble for that! Do you at all care what the man did to me? That I'm lucky to be alive? Why would you do something so stupid like that?"

"I did it because I came to believe someone really is after Mr. Taylor. I took him to your New Hampshire cabin for now because I think he'll be safe there. The police were ready to close the book in his case and accuse him of murder. I thought there was more to it than that and I think I'll be proven right. I called Ettie Williams and it turns out she spoke with someone called Luke Spiros, who told her tonight's MegaMoney winner is going to be Richard Strock. He also told her Mrs. Taylor had been murdered for her winning ticket. If that's the case, how did you happen to get the ticket, Tony?"

"Kim, you need to come home right away so we can talk. Where are you now?"

"I'm at Lottery headquarters in Hingham. I just got through talking with Mr. Modine. I told him everything Ettie told me."

"You did what! Kim, I'm serious. You need to come home right away. Don't stop anywhere. Just get in your car and drive straight to Boston."

"I'm on my way," Kim promised sensing Tony's urgency. She got into her car and pulled on to the expressway heading to Boston. Amazingly, traffic was very light and she should be able to make record time to the city.

HONK! A black Cadillac traveling directly behind Kim began to blow its horn.

What's the problem? Kim shrugged. There was more than enough room to pass.

"HONK! The driver persisted in blasting his horn.

Kim pulled into the breakdown lane to allow the car to pass.

Slowly the Cadillac began to pull alongside Kim's car to pass. But it didn't pass her. Instead the front passenger side window rolled down ever so slightly. A thin piece of metal emerged, glistening in the sunlight.

Kim's mind had barely enough time to react. Forcefully she floored the gas pedal in an attempt to put some distance between her and the black Cadillac.

BANG! A shot rang out from the metal tube. The glass making up Kim's rear view window shattered. The Cadillac put on more speed and fired again.

The shot hit Kim in the shoulder. Another shot followed, hitting her in the head. Everything went black as her Mercedes smashed through the safety barrier and hurtled down a steep, rocky, ravine at incredible speed.

Killing Ettie had left Luke badly shaken. What he needed were a couple more drinks to calm down. That always worked.

Doing his best to conceal his anxiety, Luke staggered into the Glass Slipper and ordered himself a double rum and coke. Instantly Judy spotted him and came right over.

"Hi, tiger. How's it going?"

"Fantastic," Luke growled.

"Well, you don't look at all fantastic to me," Judy started running her fingers up and down his thigh. "Let's say you and me rent a room upstairs and I show you a good time."

"Ain't got no money," Luke stated.

"That's OK, sugar. I just want to be with you. We'll pick up a bottle of wine next door and then go upstairs. What do you say?" Judy continued fondling Luke.

Despite his drunken state, Luke was getting horny. "OK," he agreed.

They bought a bottle of cheap wine and Judy brought him into a roach-infested room above the Glass Slipper. On the floor was worn-out mattress.

Luke opened the bottle of wine and took a gulp. Then he lay down on the mattress. Judy helped him undress.

"Roll on your back so I can give you a massage," Judy instructed.

"I love massages," Luke slurred. "Especially you know where."

"Oh, I won't forget that part," Judy laughed. "Though I usually like to start with the shoulders and slowly work my way down."

"Don't spend too much time on the shoulders. The other part needs it more."

Judy climbed on to the bed and sat down straddling Luke's behind. Leaning over, she began to vigorously massage his shoulders with her firm hands.

"Terrific," Luke moaned, relaxing even more. He closed his eyes and concentrated on the sensations.

"By the way, I have a message for you," Judy informed him, increasing the pressure of her massage.

"A message?" Luke mumbled dreamily. She should be getting to his private parts soon. "Who's it from?"

"It's from Mitchell," Judy snapped, reaching into her boot with her right hand. "He says you talk too much." Without giving Luke a chance to respond, Judy popped open a switchblade she had just removed from her boot. Aggressively, she plunged it into the center of Luke's back.

Luke screamed, the pain catching him by surprise. When he came to the realization of what was happening, he tried to push himself off the bed. But Judy had him pinned. Before Luke could try again, she plunged the knife into another part of his back. Like a possessed woman, she kept plunging the sharp blade into different areas of his back until Luke lay motionless. Then she climbed off the blood-spattered mattress and called Mitchell. "Ninja here," she told him. "It's done."

An hour passed. Then two. Tony felt a pulsating anxiety jerking throughout every nerve in his body as he waited for Kim to get home. She should have been here by now. Braintree was not that far away. What if Mitchell got to her?

Stop thinking like that, he told himself. Several more hours passed and by now Tony was convinced Kim had met with foul play. He picked up his cordless phone and dialed Mitchell's private number. "Vampire," he said.

"Vampire, I was going to call you," Mitchell said solemnly. "The girl knew too much. I had to get rid of her."

"No you didn't," Tony felt like crying. "You could have let me speak with her. What did you do to her?"

"Ms. Long had a most unfortunate motor vehicle accident. I'm sure you'll get over it, Vampire."

Not so. Tony knew he couldn't go on living without Kim. She was his life, his reason for living. All the money he had didn't mean anything to him without Kim. He had come to love her with all his being. Mitchell had no right to take her away from him. For that, he would make sure Mitchell paid dearly.

"Are you there, Vampire?"

"I'm here."

"And you're still with us, right? What I did to Ms. Long had to be done. Spiros had revealed too much to let her have that information. I had him taken care of a little while ago also."

"I'm still with you. Nothing can destroy my loyalty to The Group," Tony lied.

Larry Taylor yawned and glanced at his watch. It was six a.m. and he had survived his first night in the cabin. He tried going back to sleep but found he couldn't, so he got dressed and went to have a cup of coffee in the kitchen. The sunrise was beautiful he noted as he looked out the spacious window. He wished he had access to the Boston newspapers. He would have loved to read what was being written regarding his escape from Harborside. He couldn't resist a smile. Kim's stupid plan of having him dress up as a woman actually worked. Suddenly Larry heard the rumblings of a car motor getting louder. Had his hitman figured out where he was?

Tip-toeing quietly into the living room, Larry grabbed the shotgun and positioned himself in front of the kitchen's large window. A blue Lincoln pulled up into the clearing and beside the entrance to the cabin. Larry could not believe who emerged from it.

Tony nervously got out of his car. He didn't know if Larry was armed or not. How could he make it clear all he wanted to do was talk, to tell Larry the truth and then turn Mitchell and his whole organization in to the proper authorities?

"Mr. Taylor," he tried calling loudly. "I need to talk to you. I want to come clean. Kim is dead. I'm the only one who can help you now."

Kim is dead. That much Larry heard. He had nothing to lose now. He put down the shotgun and opened the front door for Tony. "How did you know I was here? What happened to Kim?"

"Let's go inside and sit down," Tony suggested. He followed Larry to the kitchen and they, two enemies, sat down opposite each other. "I've got a long story to tell."

"First of all, what happened to Kim?" Larry demanded. He had come to care about, possibly love, her.

"Kim was eliminated by order of Mitchell."

"Who?"

"Mitchell, the head of an organization I pledged my entire life to called The Group. Over the years, The Group has come to control the Massachusetts Bay Area Lottery, in particular the MegaMoney game. All winners are fixed in advance and a good portion of their winnings goes to Mitchell and The Group. Of course, if someone else also picks the same numbers, the jackpot is split and the other person gets their share. But, usually for most big drawings, a pre-determined winner is selected by The Group to claim the jackpot. It just so happens that Mr. Josh Hillman is a member of The Group. Byrant Cossetti was our pre-selected winner, but your wife also hit, cutting the jackpot in half. Mr. Hillman correctly thought that if your wife Vicki was eliminated, The Group would then have the whole one hundred million jackpot to itself."

"That's incredible," Larry's head was swimming. "How do they pull it off."

"You see, Charles Modine, the director of the Lottery, is really Mitchell, leader of The Group. He has inside information and an intimate knowledge of how to get around any security systems in place. He's a computer genius. Normally the lottery terminals are supposed to shut down after the winning numbers are announced, but Mitchell devised a way around that. He's able to alter a ticket and punch in the numbers after they are drawn."

"Who killed my wife?" Larry needed to know.

"A gentleman by the name of Luke Spiros. He was told to kill everyone in the house at the time after getting hold of the ticket. The mistake he made was in assuming you'd be home by that time also. Mitchell needed you out of the way because other than Mr. Hill, you were the only one who knew your wife had hit the MegaMoney jackpot."

"My mother and Rolando Torres. Did Luke murder them also?"

"Yes."

"And you knew everything, just as I suspected all along. You were part of all this and knew everything when you cashed in the ticket my wife was murdered for?"

"Yes. But Kim knew nothing about my involvement with The Group."

"So why are you telling me all this? Is this some plan where you tell me everything and then kill me?"

"I'm telling you everything now because of what Mitchell did to Kim. I really loved her. He had no right to take that away from me. Now I'm going to get my revenge by destroying The Group. I'm going to go to the police with you and tell them everything I know and my involvement in The Group. Charles and Martina Cooper were part of some plan Mitchell cooked up to discredit you and get you charged with murder. I'll tell the police you had nothing to do with any of these crimes and indeed, a hitman was after you all along. My aim is to make Mitchell, I mean Modine, pay dearly for killing Kim. If I can get him put away for many years, my goal will be accomplished.

EPILOGUE

Due to Tony Whiting's testimony, Charles Modine, alias Mitchell, was sentenced to serve life in prison for arranging the murders of Victoria Taylor, Rolando Torres, Helen Taylor and Lucas Spiros. Mr. Josh Hillman and various other members of The Group were handed down sentences ranging from fifteen to forty years.

For a time, the Massachusetts Bay Area Lottery was shut down until major changes could be made in management and within the system. The new director assured the Commonwealth that there was absolutely, positively no way that the new system with its new built in security measures could ever again be manipulated.

Lawrence Taylor was cleared completely of the murder charges relating to the death of his wife and Rolando Torres. He went on the lead a lonely, fruitless life. Due to the grief of losing Vicki and Kim, he never trusted himself to fall in love again.

Following testimony against The Group and its individual members, Tony Whiting entered into a witness protection program. A few months into it he decided he had suffered enough. He had accomplished what the set out to do—to destroy The Group. On New Year's Eve of that year he made one final resolution. On New Year's Day he put a gun to his head and fired.